The SALT
ANTHOLOGY **NEW**
of **WRITING**
2013

WITHDRAWN

The SALT ANTHOLOGY *of* NEW WRITING 2013

Edited by
CHRIS HAMILTON-EMERY
and JEN HAMILTON-EMERY

CROMER

PUBLISHED BY SALT PUBLISHING
12 Norwich Road, Cromer, Norfolk NR27 0AX United Kingdom

Selection © Chris Hamilton-Emery and Jen Hamilton-Emery, 2013
Individual contributions © the contributors, 2013

The right of Chris and Jen Hamilton-Emery to be identified as the editors
of this work has been asserted by them in accordance with Section 77 of
the Copyright, Designs and Patents Act 1988.

First published by Salt Publishing, 2013

Printed and bound in the United States by Lightning Source Inc.

Typeset in Paperback 9.5/14.5

ISBN 978 1 84471 919 8 paperback

1 3 5 7 9 8 6 4 2

CONTENTS

RUNNERS UP

WINNERS

WINNER BEST INDIVIDUAL SHORT STORY

JAY MERILL

AS BIRDS FLY

A GREAT FLOCK of parakeets flies over Cajamarca bound for the Southern Andes. Doña Fernanda Salvatierra Martinez sits by the window. Her eyes are fixed on the sky, dark at this moment with migrating birds. Fernanda's vision is dim now even at the best of times. She strains to see. It's her custom to stare out at the courtyard, and the street, and the tops of trees and the walls of other buildings. This marks the pattern of her day. When she was a child she saw the world with cheerful eyes. Now she looks for faults.

When the birds have passed and the sky is bright again Fernanda notices untidiness on the courtyard floor, a disorderly throng of people in the street, dead leaves in the treetops and cracks in the walls opposite. These are sights that make her shiver and groan and yet she cannot trust herself to keep away from them. For they are also the sights that fill her days and the thoughts they give rise to in her mind are the rich flavoured stew of her life. You could even say she loves the taste of the anxieties she chews round and round in her mouth when contemplating one by one each of these bars to personal happiness.

'Veta,' Fernanda calls out to her maid, and then, 'Veta,' again. Her cries are met by silence. She tries a third time, her voice now a shriek of exasperation. She waits then sucks her teeth; mutters beneath her breath. Her head sinks down into her neck, her neck into her shoulders. She hunts for the depleted strength cost her by all this calling out. 'Useless, lazy girl,' she says to herself in a wheeze. The wheeze uses up the last of the air in her throat and she coughs. Once, twice, and then she cannot stop. Veta comes up to the door of her mistress; peers through the crack. Then without a word she goes into the room, drags Fernanda forward in her seat and thumps her on the back. Once, twice. She stops.

The maid holds Fernanda in the forward position while she pats the cushions into a stiff pile. Then abruptly she tips her mistress backwards, but before the expression of terror can reach Fernanda's face her back reaches the cushions behind her and she sinks down. Relief clears her face for a second of the many myriads of complaints that lurk there on a constant basis. Veta goes across the room to the table upon which a glass stands next to a closed water jug. She pours water into it, takes it across to Fernanda who sips once or twice, the habitual crossness gradually reviving in her facial features. Veta however ignores what she sees and leaves the room at once. A minute later Fernanda calls again. 'Veta!'

Veta, who this time is waiting just outside the door marches back in, her face unsmiling.

'Yes Señora?' she intones in a bored voice which makes Fernanda crackle with pent-up irritation. 'Yes Señora, what is it now?'

'The courtyard. Look at it. What are all those boxes lying around out there? Somebody will trip over. They'll break their neck.'

'They are the new plant pots for your displays,' Veta replies in a voice of unconcern. 'They are the bottles for your preserves. They are the new cleaning brushes which have been delivered this morning, they are . . . ' 'Clear them away at once Girl, someone could trip. D'you hear me?'

'Yes Señora.' She stands where she is without moving. 'Veta, do as I tell you this minute please.'

At last Veta turns and walks through the door, goes to the courtyard. She leaves off preparing the lunch for Fernanda which she was in the middle of seeing to and the flies which were hovering near the ceiling waiting for the right moment to come and taste the food unhindered, do just this. Veta, down in the courtyard for only five minutes and removing the packages and boxes which normally would be put away by Julio the part time handyman due in this afternoon, hears the impatient tinkle of Fernanda's little hand bell, summoning her back in. She stands up straight and curses silently before going inside and up the stairs at as slow a pace as she dares.

'Where is my lunch, Girl?' the querulous voice of Fernanda squawks. 'Fetch it now, please.'

Veta goes back into the kitchen, finishes dishing the

food onto a plate. She flicks away the flies unhurriedly, with a secret laugh.

Doña Fernanda bites into her *de pollo empanada,* her thoughts uncontained by the act of eating. She is listening out for the sounds of a fracas on the street beyond the courtyard. And as with many people who listen out for something they do not wish to hear in a very short while she is rewarded. Abruptly she stops chewing. 'That is a terrible racket,' she complains to Veta, a bitten off corner of the pastie held still inside her mouth so that her words come out all muffled. Veta is standing close to her chair as though waiting for the next order. 'They must be very bad people to make such a noise on a Sunday. Today should be a day of rest, Señorita,' Fernanda scolds, reminding Veta that the woman is an outright hypocrite as the truth is she expects Veta to work morning, noon and night, Sunday the same as every other day of the week. 'Yes, they are very bad,' she agrees in a mocking voice. 'But today there is the start of Carnival and many people are on the streets.' And Veta wishes briefly and uselessly that she herself could be one of them. Doña Fernanda of course would never hear of it.

After the small satisfaction of being agreed with which Fernanda can get only very rarely from her maid, she resumes her chewing of the bit of pastie in her mouth, now soggy, and then takes a further bite. The minute she has finished eating her meal Fernanda goes across to the balcony and steps onto it. From here she gets a clear view of the unruly crowds watching for the first of the Carnival performers to appear. The sight of so many people at once gratifies her utmost desire for ill feeling and she goes grumbling away to the kitchen where Veta is now washing up the lunch plates, in order to have an audience for her expression of wrath. This consists of pacing round and round and finally taking the key down from the hook above the stove where she keeps it, so that she can lock the two of them in for safety. When the music from the Carnival rises up and assails her ears Fernanda shuts the door to the balcony so that it is stifling indoors and Veta is sure they will both faint from the heat. And of course, the rash under the skin of Fernanda's shoulders starts to burn and anti-irritation creams have to be applied, and she presses both her feet to the ground in distress causing her boils to ache.

The only one of her pet hates Fernanda has not ranted about so far are the cracks in the walls of the building opposite but Veta knows by experience that this will happen before the day is out. In the meantime Fernanda shuffles off into her bedroom for her afternoon nap which she refers to obliquely as 'going to read the papers'. Veta gives that smile of hers that isn't really a smile. She's incredulous and at the same time doesn't care what Fernanda does or says. It is bound to be something deluded, something not worth taking into account.

When evening comes but before the darkness falls, Fernanda goes to the window with her binoculars trained against the wall of the flats on the other side of the street. Her greatest source of joy and fury is seeing how these cracks in the stucco increase and deepen by the week. No one tends to them, the whole building could crumble and fall. Fernanda looks stern and unforgiving. She has a highly developed sense of the importance of property and for those whose walls fall into disrepair due to neglect she feels the most virulent contempt. 'How could they . . . . ? Imagine letting your house go to rack and ruin . . . . These people they are careless fools.' Fernanda repeats the words any number of times and yet still is hardly satisfied. Veta, now mending the edge of the lace tablecloth which got caught in the window and tore, raises her eyes, shakes her head, taps her feet.

Doña Fernanda is low in spirits if she sees leaves drying out on the trees, and the sight of leaves actually falling is an especial torment to her. She takes this as a sign that the world is going to the devil, that there is disintegration all around which will have its evil effect on those who see it happening. Yet she cannot stop, can never call a halt to thoughts like these and draw herself away, even though it means, by her own reasoning, that she will be the first to meet with trouble. She both wants to see the dried out and falling leaves and does *not* wish to see them. Yet whether she sees or does not see she thinks of the decay each time she goes out in front of her house into the courtyard over which the tops of several trees hang down. Just being there is enough to set her off to some extent. She cannot escape thinking, cannot help being aware of the worst features of this world she is living in. All the death, the decay, the loss of what as recently as last week was fine and lush – only yesterday, continually force themselves onto the attention of doña Fernanda and disturb her mind. In fact things have got so bad she now even sees dead leaves when her head is turned in towards the room, when it is night and the blinds are drawn down, when her eyes are closed. The story of perpetual decline.

It is Fernanda's special subject, the one she cannot leave behind her wherever she is, day or night, in the apartment or out of it.

Each morning when she opens her eyes she tells herself she will not think about death; she will not look at anything that reminds her of death. The trouble is that in doing this she is entrenching herself deeper and deeper. She can't let go of the anxieties and just *be*. Doña Fernanda is a woman always on her guard, who nurses the deepest suspicion that what she seeks to protect herself from will sneak in though a back door when she's looking the other way. The unfairness of this angers her and closing her eyes for a second to concentrate the better she makes a quick plea to *Our Lady of Sorrows* to intercede. Then opening her eyes again immediately as she doesn't like to think what will happen if she should fall asleep by accident, she glances slyly through the side of one eye at Veta the maid to see what the girl is up to. For the girl has to be watched. Fernanda has got it into her head Veta is untrustworthy, that she pinches food from the larder, doesn't dust the inside corners of the shelves, gives the silver only a surface buff. She sends the maid off to the kitchen to polish the spoons.

Then, 'Señorita,' Fernanda calls out suddenly in her most rasping croak. Veta, in the middle of a game on her mobile phone, comes into the room reluctantly after waiting for three minutes outside the door as a punishment. 'Yes,' she replies in disinterested tones, her eyes remote. 'Fetch me my jewel case.' For doña Fernanda loves to look at the jewels in her jewel case. Not so much because she admires the beauty of the various pieces, but to make sure nothing is missing. She tips everything out onto the table in a heap and then counts them back in again, one by one. Coming to the last piece she picks it up and stares at it. A gold brooch in the shape of a bow. Fernanda sucks her teeth then calls for Veta to pin the brooch to the collar of her dress. Each time Veta clips it on Fernanda looks into the mirror, finds the thing tips to one side or the other, tells the girl to make sure it's straight. Liking everything to be done properly is another of Fernanda's deeply rooted needs. At last she is satisfied and sends Veta away to bring some lemonade as her throat is dry again. When the girl goes out Fernanda looks at herself in the mirror with the brooch fastened to her collar, is pleased at the shine of the gold. 'Make sure that lemonade is fresh,' she screeches out, hearing the girl returning down the corridor, for being displeased with someone else at the exact same time as being pleased with herself, is one of the dualities Fernanda excels at. The girl swears under her breath as she goes into her mistress, spitting into the lemonade jug as she passes through the doorway as an expression of her disdain, thus as is usually the case, having the last unspoken word.

Out on the street a disturbance among the crowd assembled for the Carnival parade rouses the señora from her contemplation of the brooch. There comes the high pitched sound of triumphant whoops followed by discordant laughter. Doña Fernanda clicks her tongue in annoyance; goes to the balcony to see what is happening out there. She sees nothing except the dip and wheel of a certain section of the crowd, which spreads to another section, and then another, like ripples in a pond where the wind is blowing. A few arms lift up, hands grasping at air, then subside only to rise up again elsewhere. Something is happening but infuriatingly she can't see what and calls Veta over to take a look. 'Señorita, what is going on out there? What's all the bother about?' Veta looks out too but can't see either. She walks away but Fernanda calls her back. There's some new development. She holds her hand at her neck, her fingers trailing over the brooch, feeling the smoothness of the gold. A bunch of street children has detached from the rest of the crowd and are running towards the courtyard of doña Fernanda. There is a scream preparing itself in the lower part of her throat. It has not burst out yet, but Veta knows if she doesn't take action, it will. She pulls her mistress by the arm, 'Come away Señora, these are bad children. Come to your chair now.'

She coos in her most soothing voice but it does no good. The scream is already forming. Fernanda opens her mouth and it pours out from between her lips causing the maid to drop her mistress's arm and hold her ears. Even so the sound penetrates. The street kids below stop running and stare up at the balcony, laughing and jeering. Doña Fernanda is white and trembling but she holds her ground, clinging to the balcony rail with one hand to try and steady her nerves. 'How dare you come here, you riffraff. How dare you laugh at me.' She draws up all her dignity but the laughter does not stop. Now they wave and gesticulate. Fernanda feels a sense of outrage at the point blank insolence of it. But she's done with screaming. The scream she just let rip didn't achieve anything, ear piercing and terrifying as it was. And Fernanda is not one to waste her breath in vain. The children leap up as if to reach her, hollering and whooping in a chorus of glee. Then something unexpected catches Fernanda's eye, something higher up. She stares towards the balcony above her own. A long thin piece of string hangs down. 'Veta, what is that?'

Veta however has escaped to the kitchen on some excuse and does not re-appear so Fernanda moves closer to the string to investigate it for herself. As she peers upwards the shouting and cries of the kids below reaches a new height. Then before Fernanda's eyes the string twitches. Once to the left and once to the right it goes with the force of a whip. Then it coils slightly towards its tip before rising up and twining itself round the strut of the higher balcony. The kids cheer as though at the conclusion of some amazing circus act and then they run off suddenly as the first of the Carnival processions comes into view with a mighty burst of music. Fernanda looks up again. There is now no sign of the string at all but a pair of assessing gold-brown eyes are staring intently down at her. And here comes the moment when the life of doña Fernanda is to change.

The angry demand for Veta to come in from the kitchen when she's called for dissolves before it can be uttered. Fernanda opens her mouth and a smile appears instead and the monkey peering down at her from the balcony over her head, pulls back his gums and smiles back. If it *is* a smile. Fernanda herself doesn't question it. Her own smile increases. The monkey jumps down till he is near to her face. He looks closely into the recess of Fernanda's smiling mouth, lifts up his arm with one finger extending forward and taps at Fernanda's gold tooth with the nail. She knows it is the gold tooth because of the hollow metallic sound. Tap, tap, goes the fingernail of the monkey against Fernanda's tooth, and she keeps her mouth open longer than she would normally have done after smiling, to enable this tapping to continue. The monkey stares at her as if doors are being opened, dreams are being fulfilled, happiness is now possible. At last Fernanda has to close her mouth as her jaw has begun to ache. The monkey seems to understand. Fernanda steps from the balcony into the room of the flat and the monkey comes too. Of course he does. He's an opportunist. Fernanda goes and sits on her high backed chair and the monkey wanders about the place, sniffing at this and that and having a good look round. Both Fernanda and the monkey are thoroughly aware that he's moving in. There's no anxiety over this on either side. A harmony of fixed purpose already exists between them. At length the monkey jumps up onto the small table which is placed next to one of the windows. This is where an empty gilded birdcage stands. He opens the door and pokes his head inside.

At this Fernanda really begins to laugh. She opens her wide mouth to cackle and the row of little crooked teeth, which she normally prefers to hide from view, are all on show as she holds her head back and rocks to and fro. The monkey rushes across to her and once again taps at the gold tooth and then finds a second one just a little further back. He stares into the roaring cavern his small pointed face serious with musing, with questions. Veta comes in at this moment and makes a shooing noise when she sees the monkey poised close to the mouth of doña Fernanda. He waves his angular arms at her and makes a hissing sound. Fernanda sits up straight, the laughter fading quickly. 'Veta,' she says, 'Please fetch some water for this monkey. I am sure he would like to have a drink.' 'What will he drink it from?' Veta asks. Fernanda hesitates, unsure. 'Bring him the gold beaker.' There is a beaker of tarnished gold at the back of one of the cupboards in the kitchen. The kind of thing that is given to a baby at a christening. Veta fetches it and pours in water from the jug. The beaker has two handles and these seem just right for the monkey's grasp. Doña Fernanda and Veta both watch in some satisfaction as the creature gulps down the water in one go. After drinking, the monkey focuses all his attention on the goblet itself, turning it this way and that in his narrow hands, then holding onto it with one finger as he scampers across the backs of two sofas and leaps up to the small table where the birdcage stands. Next thing, the monkey opens the birdcage door, carries the beaker inside and places it at the base of one of the curved gilt struts. Then he climbs out of the cage, shuts the door, and lets out a torrent of screeches which rival the worst that Fernanda herself is capable of. She looks on in an alarm that quickly turns to delight, opens her mouth and starts laughing once again. Veta has never heard her mistress laugh before and though the laugh that comes is a little scary because it's so intense this could be because Fernanda has forgotten how to do it lightly. Things may improve. Vets supposes it's a positive development. When Fernanda laughs, her mouth open wide, her head tilted back, the monkey rushes across and stares in, close to her row of twisted teeth. Veta shoos him away again but he hisses at her at once then proceeds to tap the teeth. She notices he taps only the gold. Well, such an imposition is up to Fernanda to deal with. Veta gives her customary shrug.

Days pass comfortably. Doña Fernanda has her new companion. She has named him Manolo. This small lithe monkey with his flecked brown eyes. Manolo is adaptable and astute. He senses Fernanda's joy in him, his power in the household, her need. All the jewels in the jewel case which Manolo has an eye for are now held for safe keeping inside the birdcage. Often he is to be seen sitting on a little woollen mat Fernanda has placed for him on the table in front of the door of the cage. Sometimes he goes inside and lifts up the treasures one by one and then lies them down again with precision. No one is allowed in the vicinity of this table. Occasionally he will lead Fernanda by the hand to admire his palace of gold but if Veta should even approach Manolo will hiss, bare his teeth, and leap round the room in a state of agitation. She isn't fazed by this taboo. It's one less place to clean.

Now Fernanda goes to the market place each day. Manolo sits in a buggy and she pushes him wherever he wants to go. One day there is for sale a miniature gold woven *montera* and Manolo becomes so anxious when he sees this little hat and looks at doña Fernanda so beseechingly his head on one side, his bony fingers pressed to each side of his lovable pointed face that she allows him to try it on. He sees himself in the mirror the stallholder keeps for customers and he's ecstatic with glee. He starts nattering away, his teeth making a biting motion and snatches the hat closer to him when the stallholder attempts to take it off again. Fernanda hurriedly pays for the item and all are content. Now Monolo wears this fancy hat on their daily excursions to the market, sitting up in front of the buggy with a dignified look that makes all who see him smile. At home he guards it with the rest of his golden treasures in the birdcage while doña Fernanda Salvatierra Martinez dozes in her chair.

When days are warm and the monkey perches on the edge of the table, claps his hands, clucks like the hens in the yard, calls out to her with a sound like the cracking of a nut, Fernanda is all smiles for the joy of the world. Easily forgotten are the boils on the underside of her feet, her dimming eyes, the burning itch of her left shoulder blade, the darkness where she can only imagine sadness. She has done her struggling through days of pain, lament her only solace, has come full circle back to the brightness of life, arrived at last in the place where she first started from. As birds fly.

ARMANDO CELAYO

IF THIS WAS A LOVE STORY

IF THIS WAS a love story, I'd tell you about her nose and all the nights she kept him awake, her breathing like toilet water sucked through a sewage pipe, or all the Sunday mornings, his favorite time of the week, when she, just wearing one of his faded-soft t-shirts, would sing and dance to the songs on the radio as she watered his half-dead plants, or how she'd scribble notes onto scrap pieces of paper and leave them for him to find, or the trip they took to watch The Roots play a show down in Austin, how on the way some woman made the mistake of cutting her off, and the shit he never thought he'd hear from her lips, I'm talking ghetto-ass four-letter curses *and* old world plague-upon-your-house curses, and how this endeared her to him, or when he told her about 9/11, how for a year afterwards he was nothing but a bundle of frayed nerves and bud smoke, and how she responded by weaving her fingers with his and telling him about her father, how he used to beat and berate her for earning anything less than an 'A' on her report cards.

But as much as I want it to be, this story isn't about that.

He'd read one of her texts. Accidentally, you know – her phone kept beeping while she was in the shower. It was a grainy photo of a curved dick, from a number listed as 'Regina.' *same time next week xx*.

Something awful and uncertain ulcered in him. The next night he stayed out shooting Jim Beam long after his friends had left him at the bar; he tried to find relief in the hyssop-and-whiskey-scented company of a woman named Marcy.

He couldn't go through with it.

As he staggered home, preparing for the end, all he could think about were the hushed moments, when they were nothing but whispers and fingertip touches, and how at night, when she would rest her arm across his bare belly, how he'd place the palm of her hand over his heart.

CLAIRE ASKEW

FIRE COMES

Fire comes to the garden like a sordid thought, brought
     by a hand starfishing out
to ditch a Silk Cut filter still alight. It can't believe its
     luck: a smudge of creosote
spilled up a wall, a windless night, the brown grass stiff
     as hackles, ankle deep
and stirred by ticks that fizz and burst like cereal in
     Fire's mouth. It rises,
slides its greasy back against the fencing slats,
     unfocusses the garden in a haar
of smoke. Beyond the helpless trees somewhere a dog
     rattles awake; the air brake
of a distant night bus seethes.
Fire slides its tongue into the house's ear.

This is where the delicacies are: long flanks of cloth that
      Fire can hoover up.
Stuffed furnishings, their safety labels powerless as
      lucky charms; the carpets thick
and edible as bread. In folded quiet, Fire gums the
      skirting boards, flirts briefly
with its own reflection in the triple-mirrored gas-fire's
      front. In the hall it pauses,
shorts the fuse box; stops the shrill, pinched pinging of
      the smoke alarm and pulls
the walls down round its shoulders like a cape of dark.
      Now every downstairs room
is Fire's. The windows blow. The faces of the white goods
      melt like cheese.

Upstairs, the woman holds the house's only heartbeat in
      her clotted chest.
The varnished floorboards spit and pop while smoke
      gritty as candyfloss
redraws the room. She's coldly calm: though Fire is
      taking bites out of the white,
tiered staircase like it's cake, she can already hear the
      engines' gorgeous, strobing cry
four streets away. All she can think of, crouching down
      for air the way she learned
in school, is all those times she filled out mental lists of
      things she'd save from Fire.
The photographs, the diaries, the cat she thought she'd
      buy but never found or named.

And then the street's a discotheque of blue and red, the
        neighbours on their front steps
in their dressing gowns, the kids agape behind the nets.
And she wants none of it.
And Fire takes it all.

PEARSE MURRAY

OFF
KAIZERSGRACHT

> *... desire is born of defective knowledge ...*
> THOMAS MANN

Morning

9:00. Early May; the city trams clang with their intermit-
tent bells tracing along streets of walking figures and
moving infinities of bell ringing bicycles. An early sun
shower leaves the tram tracks with an intense glisten of
silk steel webs which seem to awaken the inhabitants into
joy. Canals of water flow against grey walls of stone in a
gentle glide of time.

9:02. At the rear courtyard of their stepped gabled row
house built *circa* 1670, Hank, 84, at his breakfast table, is
told by Heidrickje, 79, his wife of 56 years that she was
unfaithful to him when she was 30 years old and had a

two year affair with his best friend, Johannes. Johannes had committed suicide after their break-up. The cause of his suicide was mysterious to everyone but Heidrickje. This secret was pressing her to reveal itself, sensing her husband's demise. Hank smiles, and at the precise clang of a tram bell on passing in the front of their house he breathes his last breath and slips into his new and final dark.

9:04. Tall Viktor, 23, philosophy student, in a vague expectation of some drama, is setting out for his part-time job in a bookstore, tardy as usual, passes Hank's house; his eyes turn to Digna, 25, a sylph, a figure of beauty across the street going in the opposite direction on her van Gogh bicycle; his neck and head quickly follow the turn of his eyes and he suddenly walks into a black phallic bollard, stumbles to the ground and twists his ankle. Beauty can humiliate.

10:06. On the third level, adjoining Hank's house, Adrienne, 24, artist from Dublin, and Rouven, 28, artist from Munich, are lying in bed, having spent the previous night together eating a lot of magic mushroom truffles and are incoherent to each other and to the world. They will be in this state for several more hours. They have been living in this city for over two years and are trying to establish themselves as artists. They are somewhat deservedly appreciated by the elite of the art world.

11:08. A very tall colourful Swedish tourist, Henrik, architect, 55, in excited curiosity, enters the Echkof Art Gallery

five houses from Hank's house. He is viewing a series of
graphic etchings, figurative abstractions of sex, the verb.
He purchases two of them, and plans to hang them on a
white south wall in his luxury restored 19th century fourth
floor apartment in central Gothenburg. He is fond of the
CoffeShops and a frequent but discriminating visitor to
the Red Light district, being an explorer in carnal adventures and the dialects of civil sin. He is divorced and has
travelled the world in search of some beauty that continues to elude him. He has a small private practice but
the dream commission to design an art museum also
eludes him. Henrik is of private means, obtained from his
father's mining endeavours.

11:10. Six houses down from this gallery in a carriage
house attic, built in 1660, there are some mice living near
a cedar encased panel in which there are several paintings one of which a lost Vermeer rests. It is of a scene from
the window of the rear courtyard of the house depicted
in *The Little Street* and shows a maid washing clothes in a
wooden bucket. It is damaged in the right hand corner. It
is as good a painting as *View From Delft* that Marcel Proust
declared was the most beautiful painting in the world.
No one knows it was placed here shortly after it was pur-
chased in Delft by a merchant in 1675. It will remain here
for another thirty three years. If there is such a thing as
the most beautiful painting in the world someone will also
declare this of this work when it is revealed to the astonished art world.

11:12. A short and heavy-set Swiss banker, Max, aged 52

is walking past Hank's house and is somewhat lost but clear in his pursuit to visit the Rijksmuseum for the first time and see the newly restored *Woman in Blue Reading a Letter.* He has seen 27 Vermeer's of the extant 35 and it is his intent to see all the originals having discovered their calm beauty when he first was brought to visit the Mauritshuis Museum at The Hague by his guide, some-time mistress, Beatrice, 38. He was then 50 and has been feverishly travelling in between his speculating duties on foreign exchange transactions on a larger scale than these paintings of intimate domestic interiors. His discovery of Vermeer provoked him into some reflection of his hith-erto unexamined life. This pursuit, it seems, is all he lives for now as if he was deprived of these opportunities from birth, too brief a childhood, boarding school, devoid of love; he entered at the age of 22 into the grubby business of casino capital.

11:44. On the opposite end of the block of row houses at the south corner on the upper floor, 22 year old bassoon-ist, Elga, is practicing for her upcoming major recital with a wind ensemble at the Concertgebouw and she is flag-ging at a particularly difficult few bars of a piece com-posed for the group, a specially commissioned work by a composer she dislikes. It is in the key of C minor with dark murmurations of foreboding. She is nervous of her skills, fretting in fact, and is beginning to wonder if she is really suited to the performance of music, Baroque or modern. Her boyfriend, Bernard, 24, is away doing gradu-ate work in sub-atomic particle physics at Utrecht and her wish to solve the geography of love and lust is being hampered by lack of money. Her parents are recently divorced and seem to have lost interest in her, pursuing their own goals of changing careers in a new economy and their new lovers.

11:46. Heather, 22, from Chicago, has just completed her dance exercises to Arvo Pärt's *Quintettino* and Elliott Carter's *Tintinnabulations for Percussion Sextet* on a floating resilient wood floor, talcum powdered, at the second level of a dance studio located seven houses from Hank's house. She will audition with a new dance company this afternoon with these two pieces to her own choreography. She left Chicago in haste, having broken up with her lover, Cesar, 24, also a dancer of great promise. She has suffered from an over-bearing mother and feels deliriously free being 4,969 miles away from her mother's home.

11:49. Dirk, 29, has a day off from his work as an archivist at an Amsterdam museum. He is cycling with his passenger daughter, Lisa, 4, to the park from their apartment three houses from Hank's house. He is a very good father and is supportive of his wife, Silvia, 30, in her pursuit of a doctorate in economic history. In her small study she is finalizing her doctorate dissertation on seventeen century mercantile capitalism and she has worked on this for over six years, exhausting all the possible archival material in official and private records. She will inform Dirk and Lisa tonight that she is pregnant. He will be overjoyed and so will Lisa who will ask if she will have a sister or a brother.

Afternoon

3:10. Four eight year old girls, Irene, Veza, Marina and Saskia are playing hopscotch on dark red herringbone patterned pavers in a recessed area at the far end of Hank' street. A plane tree in a state of bird song frames the end of this recess. A mild argument between Veza and Irene over the colour of the chalk to be used on the 'safe' box, red or blue, is settled with the intervention of calm Marina who suggests a third compromising colour of orange, 'it is our country's colour!' Veza is the object of nine year old Harmen's gaze from a second floor window. He wonders if he will get his first kiss from her sometime soon. This evening he will watch with his father the news on television in which many conflicts in the world are reported on. He will express a wish that the world will become peaceful someday soon. His father, Peter, 45, tells him that this will only happen when hell freezes over but that we should always live in hope. Harmen is further burdened with painful desires and he will experience sleeplessness tonight, his first of many in his long life.

3:13. Viktor, now in a cast for a fractured cuboid has returned to the street and is helped by his sister, Katia, back to his apartment on the front second floor of the house adjoining Hank's house. He will not be at work for another two weeks and will read more Spinoza, play computer chess and listen to Herbie Hancock and Chick Corea while brooding on the beauty that brings pain. He will ponder for some time the absurdity of pursuing Digna and the absurdity of not. Viktor will peer out his window at 9:04 every morning in hope.

~

3:15. Adrienne and Rouven emerge for some fresh air and walk towards Rembrandtplein for food and drink. They are in love and will marry each other. They will live happily for the rest of their lives in Berlin, running an art studio where they will jointly create large scale gouache paintings, signed by both of them, as they see the world in exactly the same way. They will sell their art to the very rich, all of whom will live a mix of happy, miserable and indifferent lives.

3:16. The Swiss banker has visited Vermeer and was in a stunned state of euphoria from his lingering stare at the *Milk Maid* and the *Woman in Blue Reading a Letter*. He has now however developed a fatigue that he cannot seem to relieve even with several rests on his route back to his hotel. He is alarmed at the hammering in his heart. He thinks he should stop eating so much and has been getting very heavy over the past few months and walking in cities has not helped. Max thinks he should return to going to places by limousine. He should see a doctor as soon as he gets back to Zurich but only after he visits Dresden, Frankfurt, Berlin and Vienna to complete his journey through the art of Vermeer. He suffers a heart attack on entering the hotel off Hank's street. After a few days in an Amsterdam hospital he will be dispatched to Zurich to his wife, Ingrid, 51, and the care of the medical science that is there. He will become increasingly miserable in his fragility and will never see another Vermeer in the flesh.

～

3:17. The bassoonist ceases her practice of the commissioned work. Bernard surprises her in a visit from Utrecht. He asks how his happy and sad instrument player is. They embrace; make promises to each other in resolving their predicament of geography. She still sees travelling as a necessary condition of being a musician and this will produce a profound anxiety in Bernard. They will break up when her wind ensemble secures concert engagements that stretch out for three years of confirmed venues throughout the world. She will meet a famous violinist, Sergei, 37, and they will marry. She will improve her skills, master the lower registers of her instrument, expand her repertoire, compose and wallow in her happiness and Paris will become her base. After graduating, Bernard will take over this apartment and live in this city for the rest of his life, alone and somewhat happy in his study of quarks. He will from time to time listen to recordings of Elga's compositions and her award-winning recordings of the complete bassoon concertos of Vivaldi.

3:20. Ema, 38, Artistic Director, informs Heather that she has been accepted into the new dance company and arrangements are being made for her to obtain a work permit under a three year contract. Ema added that the company was inspired also by her choreography and there will be potential for commissioned work going her way. Heather is ecstatic and she telephones her mother who does not seem to appreciate the import of this breakthrough direction in her daughter's life and instead of a congratulatory, thrilling endorsement, asks when she will be coming home. This confirms Heather's mistrust of words and why she prefers her body to express what it is that is in her. As a result of the absence of any enthusiasm from her mother, perhaps even the absence of love, Heather will get drunk more than the celebration warrants this evening. She will injure her left knee, slipping on the stairs going up to her rented apartment. Tomorrow she will be treated by the same medical staff as Viktor was this morning. This injury will be overcome and Heather will dance her heart out for the next three years with a heavy reliance on pain killers. The long term use of these opioids will eventually kill her.

3:20. Fahri, 43, sits on the tram seat just vacated by Henrik who is now on his way to Centrum Station to catch a train to Brussels for another Gallery visit. Fahri is on his way to work at the restaurant off Kaizersgracht and will waiter to rich tourists until 11:00 PM. He will return to his rented apartment to embrace his wife, Rana, 35, and look into his three sleeping teenagers. He is miserable and wishes to return to the city of his birth and so does Rana. Their sons, Öcalan, Ayup and Cağlar love this city where they were born and are so happy that they bristle at any suggestion of a return to their parents' country with additional moans about not getting to see their favourite team, Ajax . . .

3:22. After an initial orchestration of funeral arrangements with her two sons, Franz, 52, and Jacob, 54, Heidrickje takes a brief silence of time. Gnawing into her sorrow is the image of her husband's smile. Did it mean that he always knew this secret? Was it a forgiving smile, in its waiting all these years to be told by her directly and that he was glad she finally told him? Or did he mock her and the dead Johannes in a bitter smile in the astonished realization of a whole life's relationship without truth and authenticity? That it was a smile she was certain of but she will never know of its meaning. In fact, it was a smile of pain, which sometimes occurs before death.

3:28. Silvia welcomes home Dirk and Lisa with enthusiastic embraces and kisses. She is joyfully done! Her dissertation will be defended in two weeks' time. This work will be published, translated into twenty-two languages and will be hailed as one of the great histories of the period both for its powerful analytic conceptual language in the structures and processes of human development and for its inventive historical methodology. She will gain an international reputation leading to academic promotions, frequent international conferences, guest lectures, and more publications on capitalism, capital accumulation, the economic dynamics of markets, enterprise formation and dissolution, economic power, state power, class formation, and the possibilities of a progressive redistributive world economy and justice. She is unique among historians, she will make history. Many male intellectuals will lust after her and not just for the movements in her brilliant mind. Dirk, Lisa and baby Ruud will remain happy. Silvia will be torn sometimes by the conflict between the life and the work and will have a lingering regret in not having pursued something other than that of academia.

3:50. The hopscotch game is over and the continued glistening gleam of things is assured with a series of thunderous rain showers and bursts of sun shafts which leave water-stars silvering in the air, on all the surfaces of all things in the accumulated embodied labour of this city and on all the flesh of life. Every living figure here will remember this day. The River Amstal gently sweeps through the city. This river, as with all rivers, will not sleep this evening and will remain restless as these inhabitants, in continuous states of directional anxieties, vague and certain, advance towards their own amnion sea.

SARAH-CLARE CONLON

CLEAN ME

STINKY JIM IS talking broken biscuits again. Lou stares at his lips; concentrates on making out what he's saying. The other customers are getting jittery and she needs him to calm down.

Lou nods at Jim, reaches under the counter and fishes out two speckled sky-blue and white tablets. She hands them over and he returns a head movement, the nearest he ever gets to thanking her. She watches his hunched back dwindle as, still chunnering and cussing, he drags himself across to the edge of the room.

Stinky Jim is Lou's favourite. She loves the way his filthy clothes and filthier words grate against the shiny surfaces and surgical striplighting.

She glances across at the bank of silver machines. He dribbles dirty rags into one, crowns them with the two blocks, slams the lid shut and sends coins down the slot with a final swear to launch the cycle.

Lou smiles that small smile and thinks about telling

Jim to wash his mouth out. After all, she is here to help people make everything fresh and clean and new.

PAUL McMAHON

SHROUDS

He was about six or seven, black rubbish-tip hair,
big doe-eyes, teeth driftwood-white,
a painted-on ringmaster's moustache, outstretched arm
and hand held out like a soup-kitchen ladle.
I was standing beside one of the cremation paddocks
at the burning Ghats in Varanasi. A pyre was blazing,
bruise-black smoke rose up into the vacant sky
and the sun burned down over the slow, wide Ganges
and the vast, sandy tidal plain on the far side.
Garlanded chanters in a canoe rowed a dead guru out
for river-burial, the shrouded corpse lay stiffly across
the bow like the firing arm of a crossbow.
The artful-dodger street-child tugged at the hem
of my sleeve and I looked down into his hazel eyes
to see that all my ambitions were meaningless dreams,
illusions that would vanish into smoke at the end
of my days. I felt hollow, like a bubble,
shrouded-off from anything real.

As I reached into my pocket that I kept stocked
with sweets for the street-children I glanced
to the blazing pyre – a man, a fire-warden,
was picking up an arm, by the elbow,
which had fallen out and he threw it back on top
of the furnace-orange flames. When I gave
the hazel-eyed street-child the sweet,
a chocolate éclair, he clutched it in his flycatcher-hand
and then asked me for money. I looked away –
the day before I saw him hand his coins in
to a lanky teenager who had the stern eyes
of an amateur knifer. The child shrugged-off,
examining the shrouded éclair,
its plastic wrapper a black velvety blouse,
which he opened, revealing an inner wrapper,
a white geisha-corset stuck sugar-tight against
the treacle skin which he peeled back
and gently released like a dove's wing onto the air
before he tossed the sallow toffee body
into his gaping mouth. I turned back to the paddock
and the burning pyre, its summit
of unquestioning flame – the detached arm
had landed palm up; the fingertips lightly cupping,
it had let go of all it had given or been given,

taking and being taken by
the swift-running flames –

and, in the drone of the fire,
I watched the shrouds unravel.

JONATHAN PINNOCK

DUO FOR OBOE AND VIOLIN, OP. 27

PRELUDE

September, 2022

In truth I would rather have been almost anywhere else on earth that autumn afternoon, but I couldn't help myself. I was visiting an old friend on his sixtieth birthday and it turned out that he lived nearby. And once I realised where I was, it was impossible to resist the magnetic pull of the place.

The cottage was still there, although it had been re-painted since the summer we had spent in it all those years ago. I wondered if it was still being let out, or if someone had settled there for good. I hoped they were happy there.

The bridge over the gorge was also still there: of course

it was. But it looked somehow smaller than I'd remembered. I could feel my heart pounding a powerful bolero against my chest as I stepped onto it. As I reached the centre, I began to feel unsteady on my feet, and I staggered over to the side, grabbing hold of the guardrail. I didn't want to look down, but I couldn't help myself.

I remembered arriving on the bridge that morning in a panic wondering where he'd gone to. I remembered seeing the charred pages floating in the river below and I remembered thinking to myself that surely he couldn't have gone and done anything really stupid. Then I remembered leaning over a little further and seeing, after all, that he had.

I'd known him for thirty-four years, thirty-three of them as his lover.

I (ALLEGRO CON BRIO)

October, 1978

'It's Simon, isn't it?'

'Yes, and you're – '

'Robert. What are you reading?'

'English, of course. The only subject worthy of study at this level. Did I see you at the scholars' matriculation party? At the Master's lodge?'

'No, I didn't – '

'Awful bunch of talentless wasters. I'll wager that most of them will be lucky to pick up a Third.'

'Surely – '

'I would have turned it down on principle, but I need the cash. Ma and Pa think I should be studying something dull like Engineering. For God's sake.'

'I'm reading Music.'

'How amusing. Do you compose?'

'A little. I haven't really tried – '

'I'm writing a novel. It's going to quite a sensation when it's published. Very literary, of course. I abhor the commercialisation of art, don't you?'

'Well – '

'It's so vulgar. Art does not need to be judged in the same terms as fruit and vegetables.'

'But we all have to eat.'

'My point exactly. Art aspires to greater things than mere necessity.'

'Er, right . . . so, then . . . what's your book . . . about?'

'Ah, my dear, that would be telling.'

II (ADAGIETTO)

July, 1985

'And another week bites the dust. I swear I will strangle that Beasley child if he turns up again for his lesson without his music. And that new girl, Amanda something. I don't understand how it's possible to play the piano out of tune, but she seems to manage it.'

'Maybe she plays in the cracks.'

'Maybe she does. Anyway, the portfolio's gone off to a few more agencies, so one day I might be able to give up this teaching lark. Well, it's nice to dream.'

'Isn't it just?'

'So how's the great Clapham novel coming along? You know I'm relying on it to support us in our old age, Simon.'

'Mmmm. Not so good today. I went for a walk on the common to get some inspiration, and I found an awfully nice pub that I hadn't been to before. By the time I'd finished lunch, I wasn't really in a fit state to do anything. Bit of a bugger, really.'

'Oh, you're incorrigible. Still, I expect you found plenty to write about there, eh?'

'Yes, I suppose so.'

'Anyway, it's Friday evening, and I've had enough for one week. Where's the corkscrew?'

'There's a bottle open already. Actually, maybe you'd better get another one.'

III (ANDANTE)

November, 1993

'Thanks for coming along. I know how you hate these things.'

'It's OK. You know I wouldn't have missed it for anything.'

'And you know I don't believe a word of that, Simon.'

'I think I might have nodded off during your bit. What was it you were nominated for?'

'Best music for a thirty-second commercial. For sanitary towels.'

'On which subject you are no doubt an expert – '

'It's not mandatory.'

'Well, thank the lord for that, my dear.'

'I didn't win, by the way.'

'Oh. Are you disappointed?'

'Not greatly. I only came here to show my face. Networking. You should try it.'

'What do you mean?'

'Well. See the chap over there? The woman with him is

an agent. Just struck a mega deal for some thriller writer
or other. No-one we've heard of, of course, but you know
. . .'

'I . . . no . . . no, I don't think so . . . no – '

'Are you all right?'

'Yes . . . yes . . . I'm fine. I think I might just – '

'Simon, do you really think you should be having
another drink? That's – '

'Oh, piss off and leave me alone. Go and network.'

'Simon – '

'I said, piss off.'

IV (ALLEGRO FURIOSO)

March, 2002

'I've got a new commission. A big one.'

'Good.'

'You don't sound pleased.'

'And you sound surprised?'

'OK, listen to this. There's some work for you in it, too.
If you can hold it together for long enough.'

'Oh, for fuck's sake, don't patronise me.'

'Don't you at least want to know what it is?'

'Oh, let me guess. You've been commissioned to write
this year's Eurovision effort and you want me to write the
lyrics. OK, here we go. Boom-bang-a-fucking-boom. La-
titty-la-la. Ooh ah ooh ooh ah. That do?'

'Simon, please, I'm being serious here. This is an
opportunity for you to actually write something serious
that people will pay to hear. I've been commissioned to
write an opera, and I need a libretto.'

'Well, I still feel patronised. What's the subject?'

'Ah.'

'What do you mean, ah?'

'Well, it's . . . it's . . . Princess Diana . . . Simon? Simon, please don't laugh – '

'Oh, it just gets better and better, doesn't it? Well, you're welcome to tart yourself to anyone who crawls past your kerb, but please don't start pimping for me, Robert. Princess fucking Diana. What were you thinking?'

'Do you ever want to see yourself published, Simon?'

'Oh fuck off.'

'Simon? Please?'

(Bridge Passage)

July, 2012

Simon needed some time away from everything to clean himself up. I'd made some decent money from my score for a cheesy film score – something to so with vampires or some such nonsense. It was enough to take a few months off, so we rented a little cottage deep in the country, perched on the side of a gorge. The place had no landline, and we agreed that we would not take any mobile phones with us. There was to be no internet. The only communications we would accept would be via Royal Mail, forwarded from our flat in London.

I'd had an idea for a chamber piece that I wanted to explore as well. Something personal. Something composed for its own sake, and not for some idiot of a commissioning producer. It was a duo for oboe and violin. I'd been fascinated by the idea for a while, as they were always my two favourite instruments when I was scoring for orchestra, and there were so few pieces written to show them both off together.

As it happened, it wasn't an easy task to pull off. The oboe's an awkward beast to compose for at the best of times. Even though the two instruments operate in a similar pitch range there are things you can do with a violin that you just can't do with an oboe, and getting them to work together without compromise proved to be a horrendous job. There were several times when I came close to giving up altogether.

Simon, on the other hand, found a new lease of life. Against all my advice, he had brought his bloody novel with him, but for once he actually seemed to be getting somewhere with his writing. He dried out with remarkable alacrity, and once again he became the witty, urbane man I used to know. There were many days when I staggered out of bed in the morning only to find him already beavering away at his laptop, rearranging his words with a massive smile on his face.

Even so, when he announced that he had finished it at last, and he was ready to send it off, I felt a sudden stabbing pain in my stomach. Sure, I said, go ahead. I don't think I'd ever seen him so happy, and I dreaded what would happen when his bubble was burst. Then I chided myself for thinking that, and I half-wondered if it was really me feeling threatened by my partner's potential success. But I knew, deep down, that it wasn't. And every day afterwards, my heart skipped a beat when the post arrived.

V (Lento)

September, 2012

'What's wrong?'

'Take a look. The first rejection has arrived. Ta-da.'

'Don't be downhearted, Simon. How many did you send it to? I seem to remember you going through an awful lot of ink cartridges – '

'Oh, don't worry, I'll pay – '

'I didn't mean – '

'No, seriously. I want to pay my way. When I get my first advance, I want to pay back everything I owe you. Start afresh. You know, I sat down and worked out everything I'd earnt so far from writing, Robert. It came to one hundred and sixty-seven pounds and fifty pee. And that includes a couple of school prizes.'

'Simon – '

'No. I said I'm starting afresh, Robert. I'm re-inventing myself. This is Year Zero. This is the first day of the rest of my life. Really. I'm not as upset as you think.'

Postlude

October, 2012

I'm sorry you had to find out like this, Robert, but if I'd told you what I was thinking of doing, you would have talked me out of it. You were always the practical one. But think of this as being the first thing I've done since we met that's completely succeeded in its intentions. Assuming I don't botch it, that is. If so, let's just pretend it was a cry for help, shall we?

As you've probably realised, the letter this morning brought the number of rejections to a nice round 30, and

I have decided to pack it in. Don't be angry with me. You always knew it would end up like this, didn't you?

I am stone cold sober as I write this. It's been good being clean for the last few weeks, and I've grown to appreciate what life could be like. I envy you that. But I'm scared now. I'm scared of losing that possibility, and every rejection that comes back makes me more fearful than ever.

Write something good for me, will you?

CODA

October, 2012

With the help of some of the people in the village, I hauled his body up from where it was swinging underneath the bridge. A little later the ambulance arrived to take it away for post-mortem analysis. I didn't know what to think. I really didn't. Simon had been such a part of my life, and yet I wondered if he'd really been there at all for most of it.

I felt terrible that hadn't even bothered to look at his poxy manuscript lately. It was partly out of sheer boredom with it, and partly because I didn't want to face up to the fact that he really wasn't any good. But he had been once, hadn't he? Was it my fault that he had lost it all?

And then, as I stood on the bridge, staring down into the water, that famous theme suddenly emerged out of nowhere. I took out my manuscript book and I began to scribble down the soaring, keening melody that I heard in my head. A eulogy for Simon. And that melody, transcribed note for note and completely unedited, became the prelude to my Duo.

Now I had that prelude – for solo violin – the structure of the rest of the piece fell into place. I finished it in a flurry of activity in between organising the funeral arrangements. It wasn't until a few weeks later that I realised what I'd done: I'd started out trying to compose a piece of pure, abstract music, but I'd ended up writing the story of our life together.

So it was that my Duo – or rather the prelude to it – became my pension fund. It regularly tops Classic FM polls and turns up on every single classical compilation that happens to have the words 'smooth' or 'mood' in the title. It has been used to sell mobile phones, washing powder, life assurance and yoghourt. It has won countless awards, and ten years on, I loathe the fucking thing. I like to think that Simon would have appreciated that.

TANIA HERSHMAN

A SONG FOR FALLING

SHE COMPOSED. A song for standing, a song for sitting. A suite of songs for bathing. Two songs she could not choose between for cookery. She was working on a song for falling from a great height – when he did.

And then she could not finish it.

She took all her songs and put them in the fridge. To make space, the vegetables – tomatoes and raw carrots – she spread out on the summer lawn.

She found she could not cry. She had no song yet for grief, she had thought herself too young. She had thought. Or not thought. And now she wished she had stared down at her falling song and considered. Why why why.

No more songs came, and the ones in the fridge curled around themselves, volcanic dust finding its way in to cover them.

When the grass on the lawn grew so that it hid her, hid her vegetables, almost hid the sun, a note appeared. Inside her head, which had been dry as Yellowstone. A song. Only a small small song. Only a song for breathing, for taking the next breath.

She would wait. Now that one had come, she was less unsure about a song for getting up, a song for moving through tall grass, a song for reentering the house. A song for how to live now that you know what life can do to you.

REBECCA PERRY

A GUIDE TO LOVE IN ICELANDIC

When throat lozenges stick together in a paper bag
it's like love.
There are certain risks in cooperative living,
warmth, gravitational laws, the sticky sun.

And when the light bulb pops and explodes
it's like love.
When we are naked and heart pounding in the shower,
in the dark, afraid of the being so close to water.

And it's like love
when the sun disappears for months
and when you stick cloves into an orange.

And when, in the woods, antlers fall from deer onto grass
it's like love.
To persist into spring when you have lost
some part of the whole self.

When you feel a chill and cover your feet
it's like love.
Suddenly you are in a movie, and the breeze from an open
window is not real, the walls are paper, the food is plastic.

And it's like love
when a train stops dead in a tunnel
and when a beloved cat suddenly shows its claws.

And when tar is compressed into uniform blocks
it's like love.
The air is choking and though the blocks are
gold bullion shape, there is nothing at all spectacular in it.

When you fall down the stairs
it's like love
and when you are soaked through to the bones,
your clothes are deadweight and the radiators click to life.

RUNNERS UP

JENNA BUTLER

THIS RAIN

brings with it the scent of rain-soaked lilac, lemon lily.
    Bruised
skirts of thunderclouds drop their wet hems over this
    prairie. It rains
and the ditches brim, rains
and the water rises like ire amongst the willows.
What we say and do not say. The heart
incandescent, riverine with distance.

~

lilt like this: sound
of droplets from leaves
    gift gift   gift

JOANNA CAMPBELL

FOLLOWING CANDACE

ON OUR LAST day in Linden Avenue, Mother taught me how to make fritters and we finished the bandaging after two weeks of work on it. The home-school authority would nod with approval that our timetable included Cookery and First Aid. An early finish for the funeral was acceptable too, especially in the circumstances.

Mother's breadstick bones were splintering with age. And brick by brick workmen were dismantling our avenue. At the far end we could see the arm of the tower-crane beckoning. We had packed most of our belongings. Only the polished jars, some cooking equipment and the tools spread out on the white towel remained.

A thin sliver of a flat was waiting for us. The block shifted in high wind, people said. I dreamed that one day Mother would cup me in her hands like a dove, open the slitty window and release me to some picture-book swoop of bosomy hills and glitter-trail rivers. She closed our curtains two weeks ago. Some mornings I pushed them aside to see the shining avenue, metallic from the sun or steaming patent-leather from the rain. The line of trees rasped and clinked in the autumn wind like old gold pouring into a tomb. All summer long they had waited like heavy new mothers, teeming with life.

When my father and I weaved between their straight trunks on our last walk, we bestowed upon each the name and qualities of a goddess. The nearest to our house was Candace. She led an army of ten thousand rebels against the Roman occupation of Egypt. Ament was the furthest. She lived in a tree on the fringe of a desert and welcomed the dead with bread and water, all the time watching the gates to the underworld. The spells of Nephthys guided them through it.

Nephthys, protector of the dead and their further adventures through the underworld, like some dark comic-book heroine. Mother had called from a window and reminded us to honour her too. No time remained to name a tree after her sister, Isis, symbol of rebirth and daylight.

Father was holding my hand, his fingers lighter than a rainless leaf.

'I don't wish to continue,' he said. 'No further. No more.'

During his final night I watched his face grow smooth, those last words circling in my head like an enchantment. He pressed a piece of paper, a healing prayer perhaps, into my hand when Mother was lighting candles. I hid it in my drawer of school socks for the days ahead.

Soon the lindens would fall, their grace sawed to a

stump in a heartbeat. Worms were burrowing deep to escape the bulldozers. The school bell would never echo through the windows of the avenue again. And I would never race the length of the field, my legs gleefully trussed to another girls' legs, in the shadow of the russet walls. The new Saver-Smart would smother the entire area.

I was almost alone.

Linden School was a watchful building, its red stone grown from the damp clay like a camellia, the roots scoring through the soil like white rivers. When Mother was a mute brown child among cream-faced girls plucking at the serpent coil of her plaits, Linden School welcomed her.

The school was my temple. It cherished every obedient girl. We all wanted to stay forever. The world loomed huge and filthy.

Now the school had gone, Mother kept me at home. The new school in the city would make me lick the mud from my hockey-boots, she told me.

I wanted to taste that living mud. I was afraid of being entombed. The last two weeks since Father died were wrapping around me like a sheath tightening its grip every day.

Mother lit our long evenings with candles and at night she curled on the floor by my sleeping-bag. She vanished and reappeared as the flame on the dressing-table leapt in the dark. The sighs slipping from her sleep disturbed my dreams, leading me through slow-winding seas that deepened into blood-red wombs.

I slithered out of the quilted nylon and sat on the sill to watch the reflection of the crane's lights winking in puddles. The night was the temple of Nephthys. Mother often stirred and once I turned to see her finger pointing at me just before the candle-stub sank into its own pool.

'Let's begin our cookery lesson,' Mother said on that last day. 'Then we shall have something special to serve guests after the funeral.'

We prepared the utensils, laying them out on a clean tea-towel on the white kitchen surface. I filled the largest saucepan with water and added scoops of salt for soaking. We whisked the batter, taking it in turns. I chopped the onions and a large carrot. Mother didn't like to relinquish control, but Father's death had left her weaker. She hoped to fill me with strength for the tasks required of Nephthys.

'This will nourish you, Safiya. Full of good cholesterol and higher in fat than you would believe!'

I was unsure about this recipe now. Like most girls of my age, I sought slenderness. My mother was trying to fatten me with fritters.

I picked up the rubber spatula and eased the uncombined flour from the edges of the basin. Mother scissored in chives. I floated a bay-leaf and six peppercorns in the brine. The water rose to the boil.

The saucepan was too heavy for her to lift and drain the salty water. She gave me instructions and I obeyed until my arms hung limp. At last we were ready to lift out the cooked brain with a slotted spoon, mixing it with beaten egg to achieve a firm texture. Mother was smiling at me as our spoons wound the egg through the claggy mixture that squelched and wheezed like rubber boots in a quagmire. I looked away, trying to breathe only the garden smell of boiled herb and onion.

We rolled the brain in our hands, forming small cakes to dip in the batter and deep-fry until the fritters turned crisp and yellow. Mother held out a finger crowned with a fleck of the mixture.

'Lick this, Safiya,' she said, the finger in front of my face.

I stepped back. The texture of brain slithered in the mouth like silken custard. But my obedient tongue reached out and curled round the speck. Mother withdrew her cleaned fingertip, her smile stretched like a tiger's.

'Good?'

'Very good. Yes.'

At the wake I would say the fritters were a favourite family recipe. Cheese and onion, perhaps, would ring true.

Mother dressed the table with a blinding-white cloth. The folds over the corners looked blue-tinged. Nothing can be pure white. A hint of another hue has to creep in.

'It looks blue, Mother,' I said.

She whisked it off the table and pummelled it in the kitchen sink. A goddess must have lent her the strength. She marched it to the launderette on the corner to watch it leap and flail in the hot air of the drier.

I began the First Aid Class. Unaided. The solitude rolled a weight off me like the August sun fries away the morning cloud haze. I could breathe, I could think, I could see.

No one at school had lived like this. And now I couldn't even exist on the edge of their lives. The darkness of death cornered me in the house. And the long passage through deeper darkness to eternal life was a journey I believed in no longer.

'No more. No further,' my father had said. The words threaded like beads on unknotted string. No more of this world. Or no more after it.

I remembered the new air on our last walk and how he said I should lift my face to it.

White sheets shed their tiny particles as I snipped them into long strips. Wedges of sun pressed through the blind and trapped the linen dust-motes, set them spinning.

As I worked, I listened to the rumble of the heavy machinery grating the avenue to fine rubble. I had almost finished one neat toe bandage when Mother came in.

'They were taking out the plastic chairs and dismantling the fittings while the cloth dried. I was the only person there. Maybe the last. The manager's child was writing a sign: Thanking all our loyal customers.' Mother sank into a chair. We listened to the lorries, to the whine of the crane's swinging arm, to the click of the kitchen-clock. I saw the long hand swipe another minute.

'Let us move fast,' Mother said. 'Another layer of bandages, Safiya. The next toe, please.'

Father still smelt clean from the washing, the rinsing in wine, the massage of sweet oil. Bacteria can still thrive after the passing of their host. My deft palms and her slow fingertips had oiled him after death, hers shaking as they anointed each dear crease or traced a well-loved line within his skin. Sometimes her finger pressed the oil onto her own lips. She skated them against his papery cheek. The rich smell of palm still pervaded the house.

We had placed the sterilised tools in a row on a white towel and we cut his left side with care, removing each organ with grace and precision for storing in the jars with animal heads for lids. He had fired them all at the Technical College's Wednesday evening pottery classes. But he was too ill to glaze them. So Mother and I brushed on the sheen for him while he gave us his gentle smile.

Soon after death Mother had inserted a long thin hook through his nostril to break his brain, enabling us to coax it down and out of his nose. It took time, but we were patient, removing every piece with care and placing it all in a good freezer-bag.

The bandaging took time because we wrapped his head, neck, fingers and toes as separate entities, then the limbs, several times over. He was a small man, but we took care to make the mummification perfect.

Today we bound the arms and legs together, placing a scroll inscribed with words from the Book of the Dead between his cottony hands, sturdier now from the layers of bandage. The spells would ward off evil spirits hindering his journey through the underworld.

'He is preserved and sanitised to perfection,' Mother announced, as we went to the kitchen to check the frying-pan. She seemed stronger now, younger, as if the fresh white linen and gleaming oils had purified her own soul. 'Safiya, you and I are protected from anguish now. His good heart is now travelling towards the clear light of eternity.'

I had dug a hole in the garden, where a bank of lilies had finished blooming. Saver-Smart would not need to churn the earth there for their foundations. We had scrutinised the plans. Our little strip of territory would form part of the planted area required by the planning authority to provide greenery, together with a slatted bench and stone litter-bin with cigarette-snubber. The supermarket would rise in a matter of weeks once the whole of Linden Avenue was removed.

Mother and Father had decided his death-chamber should be somewhere sacred, somewhere no one could disturb again. There was no point coring out some beautiful land that would be sacrificed one day, dragging out his pure soul and interrupting its quest.

'Safiya, the guests will arrive soon. They'll help us carry Father. The manager of Saver-Smart is going to say a few words at the graveside. Gather the jars, will you, dear?'

I caressed the jackal-head lid of the jar containing his stomach. I kissed Hapi, the baboon-head that housed his lungs. The cancer had intruded there first.

'Safiya, I have told you about Nephthys, the goddess of the mortuary. She protects Hapi, helps him to guard Father's ailing lungs.'

Mother placed a hand on my shoulder. No more words were needed. She turned to flip the fritters with her fish-slice. She rested each one on absorbent paper. I arranged them on a platter in the middle of the table.

I pushed the curtains back an inch to look through the window. The workmen held back the tape barrier for guests to pick their way through the rubble of Linden Avenue. I recognised the manager of Saver-Smart. Mother had promised to keep the occasion very private, just trusted friends, so that future customers would not 'get spooked' as he had first suggested might be the case.

The garden was still our land, ours for a while longer. He respected that. He was a former pupil of Linden School. He knew how monstrous life outside could be.

But as soon as I saw him stride along and catch my eye, I knew I would soon wear the red-striped uniform and stack the Saver-Smart shelves with jars and bottles in the section overlooking the patch of green.

Mother called me. The food was ready. Father was waiting. The guests were clattering up the path. I began to close the curtains. I'd never be able to leave now.

But I stayed at the window for one moment longer. Candace, the leader of the rebel army and the next in line to fall, was swaying. Her branches stretched like arms towards me, as if in some prosaic prayer always known to the avenue. Her leaves stirred, the flimsy rustle of old gold. In my pocket my father's piece of paper whispered to me. I had looked at it at last this morning. It showed a bank account number with my name. It told me to keep my feet on the ground and I laughed like any schoolgirl at the irony that this pass to the future had been nestling in my sock drawer.

And I remembered more of my lessons about Neph-thys; that she was also goddess of the air and she was a wild bird created by air and she was the source of rain and the Nile river.

Her sister Isis was the symbol of dawn, birth and growth; Nephthys depicted night, death and decay. But one was not the reverse of the other, my father had told me. They were different reflections of the same reality, all bound with life.

I opened the door to the mourners and walked past

them all. I told them about the fritters so they could be clear about the contents and make their own choice whether to eat them. And I ran along Linden Avenue in the sun until I was one heart bursting.

PHILLIP CRYMBLE

BUT SERIOUSLY, FOLKS . . .

Dish soap mixed with carbon-filtered water in a dime store

Chinese bowl, a dash of methylated spirits, rags for wicking,
and the hole-punched Joe Walsh gatefold that I bought for next

to nothing at a junk shop out in Parkdale on our holiday back

home. Like an atheist in vestments come to shepherd in a soul,
I rinse the grayish A-side in a basin — place the newly wetted

record down on muslin — wash the flaking cells and skin oils

from my fingers using numbered strokes. Ritual impositions
run to ashes, hands and cloaks — no mention of a homemade

salve for vinyl — how to remedy a verdigris of mold — relieve

endemic artifacts on playback — free the walls and troughs
from dust — ingrained tobacco smoke. In a slow decaying

orbit from the run-in to the dead wax codes, I work the soapy

mixture to a lather — track and gently loose bacterial deposits,
grit, and other aggregations fixed like barnacles on flotsam

or the keels of oceangoing boats. As if studying the features

of some primitive sonography, or glyphs incised on polished
stone, I read and half-identify an episodic storyline of squalor —

let my fingers ride the surface like a contoured diamond stylus

built for colourless retrieval — finer contact — widening
what's disclosed. I lift it at the spindle hole. Wiped clean,

hand-dried and polished to a dark, refractive glow, it holds

and throws the incidental daylight like a mirror — leads me
absentmindedly to Ovid. Not Narcissus, but the heart-sick,

wifeless Cypriot, his misanthropy and wishfulness, the snowy

necks of heifers — how a man might come to worship things
he's made, and what it means to own. I cue track eight. Turn

all the lights down low. The opening kick and snare of *Life's*

Been Good waits like a vagabond for Godot — Carl Sagan's golden record in the interstellar cold — a fossil at a dig

site — dreaming of the bone brush — ready to be known.

PETER DANIELS

BLOB POLITICS

The flags shiver for the spell of sun on the toy brick
      riverside buildings
under which the tunnelling continues: structural
      decisions made too late
and for the wrong reasons, but made to push the people
      through, smoothly
under the brimming river of institutional tea that carries
      the city
in its processional float – and someone has to be placed
      in charge of this trainset,
this whole pile of Lego: one organism out of the bag, a
      being whose preferences
represent the choice of choice. Chosen for functionality,
      for comfort, for magic.

And in the broad aorta through all our shared body,
      whose is
the adrenalin giving the message? Which lovely skin
      among us

has the nerve endings to be gratified, the targeted
     service end-user?

Feel glad for the pleasures of the city, for which we fall
     back in satisfaction
after the delay, the sighing and tetching of tongues –
     patient with our own
stuck impatience to make our small impossible goals
     work, by starting
on the buildup of minor interactions, the single-minded
     concerns of cells,
yes, of molecules, inside this heap, this blob crossed by
     a wiggle of mud.

TIM ERICKSON

VIA APPIA

It is a design
  of man
    pacing out the square-footage of the footpaths

      No pattern
      No volume without mind

A thunderbolt is comprised of air
      No thunderbolt without mind
        Reports
       Concuss and echo
       In our arrangement of the world
             ours
          No pattern
          But expedience
   Tamps the deer trail flat
   Over which we poured our asphalt

We walk on that

KEVLIN HENNEY

A HIGHER CALLING

SWIRLS AND SPIRALS, flowing lines and suggestive curves, Henry circled and embraced the sheet with one arm while the pen in the other danced across the page. A picture emerged from the pirouettes and glissades. Short on materials, short on time, steeped in inspiration. This was art. This was passion. This was love.

Henry had never felt so oppressed yet so free. No computer, no phone, no talking. The afternoon had been cleared of everyday distractions. He was alone with silence, alone with pen and paper, alone with thoughts of Margaret.

The imaginings of what lay beneath the white blouse. It was certainly more than he remembered in primary school, but perhaps not as much as the pneumatic, barely clad, advert-haired figure on the page before him. A class-mate for so long, but only this year had the progressive changes sculpted in her by adolescence caught up with him, caught the changes within him, caught him.

'Five minutes!'

Henry looked over to the next desk. Ralph's expression was as blank as the page before him. Two rows in front, the back of Margaret's head moved in time with the intensity of her writing.

Henry embossed her name in Celtic lettering, cross-hatched relief beneath the fantasy-scape of swords and unicorns, of the wielder and rider, of idealised form and magical proportions.

'Pens down, please!'

He had not even dignified the GCSE maths paper by turning it over. His was a higher calling.

This was art. This was passion. This was love.

ANNEMARIE HOEVE

AN ACQUIRED TASTE

ONCE SHE WAS served a sliver of pickled beef tongue as an *amuse* in a fancy French restaurant. Not wanting to be rude, she dutifully put every morsel into her mouth and swallowed until the plate was empty. Strangely, it didn't taste like meat at all. Instead, an explosion of fresh spring grass and buttercups danced on her tongue, clover tickled her palate and she was left with an exquisite aftertaste of dandelions in full bloom. After that she could never pass a pasture without an intense urge to graze.

DANIELLE MCLAUGHLIN

CLOCK

MY AUNT'S FLAT is like the inside of a clock: small, shining, exact. A place of things impeccably ordered. Silver teaspoons with filigree handles; a pin cushion with a hundred pearl-headed pins; gold-rimmed china cups.

My aunt trails a finger across the bruise on my temple, but she does not ask, not yet. The asking will come later. 'I could have met you at the station,' she says, taking my suitcase, 'I could have helped.'

I sit on her sofa with its row of red velvet cushions. I think I hear a soft whirring, like cogs going into motion. I listen for the tick, the tock, but it is my aunt boiling the kettle to make tea.

When she opens the fridge, I glimpse a plate of raw meat: a swollen, purple ox tongue from the market, a sheep's heart with its marbling of fat.

Here, in this flat, my aunt makes time for me. We negotiate each other within the safe confines of its walls: me, striding and jarring, she, meticulous and precise. Big hand, little hand.

I am frightened as a wounded bird, wings clipped,

spirit broken. In the days to come, my aunt will feed me slivers of heart and tongue. She will wind me until I am once more ready for flight. And on the appointed hour she will watch me burst forth, fly beyond her walls, primed for song.

C. S. MEE

FRENCH LESSONS

WHILE HIS PEERS spent their first university summer trotting around South-East Asia trying to find themselves, Daniel Maddocks sat in his parents' garden, smug in the knowledge that life was without meaning and existence pointless. Stretched out on a sun lounger he read Jean-Paul Sartre's *La nausée* and focused on developing his personal philosophy. Although, at nineteen, he was yet to experience the true anguish of nothingness, he was convinced that after a few more months on the sun lounger, he would achieve an authentic state of existential nausea.

'Are you just going to sit here all day?'

Dan's mother Denise was back from the nursing home and stood over him in archetypal matron pose, hands on hips.

He gestured for her to move. 'You're blocking the sun.'

'You've had enough vitamin D today. You were sitting here this morning when I left for work. How long are you going to stay like this?'

Dan looked at his watch. 'Weather permitting, three months.'

'Aren't you going to do anything this summer?'

'I'm very busy.' He waved *La nausée* at her. Dürer's *Melancholia* slouched on the cover like a moody teenager.

She folded her arms. 'I'm glad to see you're studying, but you're not spending the whole summer reading. Why don't you get a job or do something useful?'

'I am doing something useful. The results may not be visible, but not everything useful can be measured in pounds sterling.'

His mother sighed. 'I saw Janet today.'

'Who?'

'Janet Donovan, Nicola and Simon's mum. She told me Nicola's volunteering in Africa this summer.'

Dan rolled his eyes. 'What's she doing this year? Irrigating orphans? Vaccinating elephants?'

'Don't be silly. She's building a well.' Denise paused. 'Or a hospital . . . or a well in a hospital . . .'

'So?'

'So, why aren't you . . .'

' . . . More like Nicola Donovan?'

'That's not what I was going to say.'

'You know I *chose* not to go to Cambridge.'

Denise sat down in the grass. 'You were well paid when you worked at the home.'

'Don't even begin to suggest the home.'

She remembered overhearing one of the residents asking a nurse about the miserable young man lurking in the breakfast room. Perhaps the nursing home was not the best place for her son.

'So you're just going to sit here?'

'Three months, I told you.'

'Are you going to eat during these three months?'

'Are you going to charge me rent?'

'No love, but I do want you to do something.'

'I'll mow the dishes, vacuum the lawn, wash the carpet, whatever you want.'

'There's something else I want you to do. Janet's worried about Simon.'

'What's wrong with him?'

'He failed some of his mock GCSEs.'

'Takes after his sister then.'

'Don't be sarcastic. Simon's a nice lad, he's just not exactly . . .'

'Oxbridge material? How tragic for them.'

'He's having a hard time with French. Janet thinks it would be good for him to get some tutoring.'

She threw him a significant look and he stared at her in horror. 'No way Mum, absolutely no way. I need this summer to develop ideologically.'

Denise pushed herself up and started towards the house.

'It's that or the home, love. Your choice.'

Janet answered the door with a smile. She'd put on weight.

'Daniel, you've grown into quite a young man since I last saw you.'

He was tempted to return the compliment.

She sent him upstairs to Simon's bedroom. It was strewn with stale clothes and the air was thick with a familiar mustiness. Simon was sitting on his bed, all acne and embarrassment. Dan looked at him with disgust and went straight to the window, pulling it open with some difficulty. While the air circulated, he took a packet of cigarettes from his pocket and lit up. Simon eyed the pack and Dan started to offer him one, but hesitated.

'I suppose your Mum's about to walk in with a tray of tea and biscuits or something.'

On cue the door opened and Janet strode in carrying a tray of tea and biscuits.

Dan just had time to drop his cigarette out of the window and slip the packet back in his pocket. Janet pretended not to notice the smell of smoke, as she was accustomed to ignoring the odours lurking beneath it.

'Well Daniel, you must be a good influence, that window hasn't been opened for about five years.'

Simon scowled and Janet set down her tray.

'I thought you might need some brain food.' She beamed and left them.

Dan was hungry. He eyed the solid brown matter on the plate. 'What are these?'

'Homemade wholemeal scones.' Simon didn't touch them.

Dan picked one up and was surprised by its weight.

Simon grimaced. 'My Mum's gone crazy about baking. Nicky had to go to Africa to escape.'

Dan tried to bite the scone and his teeth met something tougher than enamel.

'Jesus! What the fuck are these made of?'

'I think she read that concrete is high in fibre.'

Dan laughed and Simon seemed pleased. They lit up and lightened up.

'So, parlons français, I guess,' Dan started.

'Er, oui.' Simon's accent didn't give Dan much to hope for.

'Alors . . . ' He tried to think of something to say. 'Qu'est-ce que tu as fait ce weekend?'

Silence.

'What did you do at the weekend?'

After a long pause Simon managed, 'Je jouer football.'

No wonder he'd failed his mock GCSE. How could anyone be so bad at a language he had studied for four years? French had always been easy for Dan, the words clicked into place and he spent most of his time in class trying to catch out his teachers or flirting with the language assistant.

'Have you got a textbook or something?'

Simon produced a battered copy of *Aujourd'hui* and Dan flicked through it hoping for inspiration. The chapters followed the Bernard family as they bought baguettes, ate camembert and cycled around Paris in their berets.

'J'aime beaucoup la tour Eiffel, c'est chouette,' Dan read. 'Zut alors, j'ai oublié mon passeport.' No wonder Simon was crap at French. The summer was going to be long. Dan considered ways of escaping the lessons, but memories of the nursing home convinced him to make some effort.

'We'd better start at the beginning. Sounds like you need some practice at verbs.'

Dan took a fresh sheet of paper, thought for a moment, then wrote down *baiser*.

Simon looked over. 'Doesn't that mean kiss?'

Thank God, the kid knows something. 'Yeah, kiss as a noun, but it's also a verb – to fuck.'

'Kiss and fuck are the same word?'

Dan shrugged. 'It's French, what do you expect?'

He wrote out the declension of *baiser*, reading as he went, 'Je baise – I fuck, tu baises – you fuck, il/elle baise – he/she fucks . . .'

Simon seemed to take an interest; he recited the whole verb and grinned. 'Je baise Katie Simmons.'

'Who's Katie Simmons?'

Simon blushed. 'She's just this girl in my class.'

'Sounds like a case for the hypothetical, but let's keep things simple for the moment.'

Back home that evening, when Denise asked her son how the first lesson had gone he scowled and complained, 'It's such a waste of my time. Simon can barely articulate in English, he's never going to remember any French.'

'Janet and I have agreed on three lessons a week, but perhaps you'll need more then?'

Dan looked at his mother in dismay. 'Three lessons a week? I can't believe you're making me do this.'

Wednesday afternoon found him back in the stale air of Simon's bedroom. Dan expected to have to start from scratch, but was surprised by how much of *baiser* Simon could remember.

Dan tested him with another verb. *Enculer*, he wrote. 'So much more satisfying and literal than bugger. 'En' 'cul', it's really *in* the arse.' He accompanied this with a hand gesture to get the point across.

Simon quickly mastered the declension of *enculer* and they moved on to other verbs. Dan decided he should impart some cultural knowledge. 'When the French are pissed off with something, it makes them shit.' He wrote out *chier*. *Ça me fait chier*, he added, thinking 'tu me fais chier', and made the bold move of introducing object pronouns and the irregular verb *faire*, so they could practice saying that different things made different people shit.

They dwelled at length on the possibilities of *foutre* and Dan took the opportunity to teach imperatives which broadened their expressive range considerably.

"Va te faire foutre', 'fuck off' or more literally 'go get yourself fucked'. If you want to be polite you can use the 'vous' form: 'allez vous faire foutre'. Another useful command with foutre is 'fous-moi la paix', 'leave me in peace', but again foutre gives it a nice emphasis that's lacking in the translation. Once more, 'foutez-moi la paix' would be more polite. You can also use foutre to talk about yourself, 'je m'en fous', 'I don't give a fuck'.'

'Je m'en fous,' Simon repeated attentively.

Over the following weeks they covered the basics of French grammar and although Simon lacked Dan's aptitude for the language, he seemed to retain more than his tutor had expected. Dan resented every minute he was forced to spend in Simon's company, but he felt that if the boy at least remembered something then his time was not completely wasted.

Soon Dan had to face the fact that although Simon was developing a sophisticated slang repertoire, they had not covered much of the vocabulary required by the GCSE syllabus. He returned reluctantly to *Aujourd'hui* and opened a chapter at random to find a list of animals. Dan pondered ways of involving animals in the phrases they had worked on.

'Who's your nemesis?' he asked Simon.

'My what?'

'Your worst enemy, the guy you really hate.'

'Oh, Nathan Gadmore, he's such a dick.' Simon brightened and added, 'il me fait chier.'

'Okay,' said Dan, 'so how do you say 'Nathan Gadmore fucks dogs'?'

They worked their way through the list of animals, learning as they went, and writing down examples. Nathan Gadmore fucked all the domestic pets, the farmyard livestock and then moved on to the zoo. He fucked some of them in the arse, for variety of vocabulary, and even fucked himself in the arse with some of the smaller ones, which provided an excellent opportunity to practice reflexive verbs.

At the end of the lesson Dan flicked through *Aujourd'hui*, to see where they should go next. The following chapter introduced fruit and vegetables and he figured they could continue in a similar vein.

As the summer progressed they worked their way through the GCSE vocabulary lists and Dan became quite proud of his ability to twist each word to their needs without having to return to the dull antics of the Bernard family. In fact the Bernards proved useful, departing from their usual script to have orgies, which reinforced the names for different members of the family, parts of the body, pieces of furniture and prepositions. Sometimes these took place in the past tense or the future, occasionally they went on trips to have sex in different civic and geographical locations. Katie Simmons also made a reappearance and her attributes were detailed with a long list of adjectives. She was undressed, item by item, and then they revised parts of the body again.

One Monday in August, as Dan was about to set out for the lesson, he got a text from Simon cancelling the class and saying something about being *dans la merde*. Dan shrugged, grateful for the free day to focus on his reading. The British summer had returned to usual form and he had abandoned the sun lounger for the living-room sofa. He settled down to read, but found it hard to concentrate and had an unproductive day.

That evening his mother asked, for the first time in weeks, how the lessons were going.

'Not bad. Simon's picked up a lot.'

'And what are you teaching him?'

'French. That's what I'm supposed to be teaching isn't it?'

'GCSE French?'

'Yeah. Where are you going with this?'

'I just had a phone call from Janet. Greg, her husband, found some of Simon's French notes and it seems he was not very impressed by the content.'

'If he knows French then why hasn't he been teaching Simon all this time?'

'I don't think he can speak French, I think he looked it up on the internet.'

Dan laughed. 'If he Googled 'Nathan Gadmore s'encule avec un hamster' he must have got some interesting hits.'

Denise tried to look serious. 'Greg's pretty angry about it.'

'Simon cancelled the lesson today.'

'Janet told me Greg wants all the lessons cancelled.'

'What? I don't believe it, we were actually getting somewhere. I was just trying to make it interesting.'

Denise hid her smile. 'Love, don't take it to heart. It's not just about the lessons, I think, there's also the guilt of a father who doesn't spend much time with his son.'

'Why is that my problem? Honestly Mum, what's the point? You try to do something for someone and this is the thanks you get.'

Denise had assumed that Dan would leap at the chance to quit, but she didn't say so. Instead she suggested they leave things for a week and let Greg calm down. Dan and Simon exchanged a few colourful text messages, but it wasn't a good medium for lessons. The week dragged and Dan made slow progress on his philosophy.

At the weekend he asked Denise if she had spoken to Janet yet.

'Would you like to continue?' she asked.

'Well . . . whatever . . . I guess it's a shame to stop now Simon's getting somewhere. He was crap to start with. Anyway, I didn't mean to get him into trouble. Whatever . . .'

Denise called Janet and the mothers decided on a resolution. They would tell Greg that Simon had a new tutor, but he would come to Dan's house and would keep his notes out of his father's sight. Neither mother made any comment to either son about the content of the lessons.

Their classes continued uninterrupted for the rest of the summer. Dan reinforced the basics, covered most of the vocabulary in *Aujourd'hui* and nurtured in Simon a highly developed capacity for insulting French speakers the world over.

A cool afternoon in late September found Dan back at university, strolling round the Societies Fair in the Student Union. The Freshers stood out a mile, with their recently ironed clothes, and Dan, wandering aloof through the eager crowds, asked himself for the nth time why he was bothering with the fair.

His mobile bleeped with a text from Simon, who was several weeks into his school term. He had got a B+ and a detention for his first French composition. Dan smiled, warm with an unfamiliar glow.

The stalls at the fair bubbled with the noise of over-enthusiasm. Dan eyed the different societies and clubs with disdain: the role-playing guild, with its huddle of pasty attendants; the sports clubs, with their jostle of rugby-shirted blokes and wiry women. He walked swiftly past his polo-necked peers at the Philosophy Club and tried to extricate himself from a confused conversation with someone from the Russian Society who mistook him for a compatriot.

As Dan tried to make his way to an exit, his path was blocked by another manic volunteer.

'What are you studying?' the volunteer asked, waving a clipboard at him.

'French and Philosophy and no, I'm not interested.'

'Wow! That's so cool. We need French volunteers.'

'What for?'

'We match up students with GCSE and A-level pupils

in local schools to help tutor them for their exams. It's a great way to . . .'

'No way, I've just spent a whole summer doing that. Never again.'

Dan tried to push past the volunteer but he thrust the sign-up list at him. 'Look, we don't have anyone for French.'

'What?'

Dan looked at the lists. Chemistry, geography, English and biology were almost full, maths ran onto another page, while French was empty.

'Not a single person? For fuck's sake.' Dan snatched the pen from the volunteer. 'No wonder everyone is so crap at French.' He furiously wrote down his name and email address, shoved the clipboard back at the bemused volunteer and marched off muttering something about how attitudes to language learning made him shit.

ALBAN MILES

FISH EYES

WHEN I WAS a little girl, I crawled between the legs of
the kitchen table and put a fish eye in my mouth like it
was a sweet.

My mother was forty-two when I was born. She had the
palest green eyes, like pieces of green glass washed and
washed by the sea, and I was always mysterious to her. I
am a child of her middle age, youngest of five and one too
many. The fish eyes story was a way that she had to fix me.

When I was twelve she told Elizabeth Hollis's mother
on the front porch of our house. A few weeks later the boys
at Youth Orchestra started calling me *fish eyes, fish breath*.
I had to stop going to Youth Orchestra that summer.

My father taught at an art college but I believe he
never came to terms with the idea that he wasn't a pro-
fessional artist. When I got home from school he was up
in his studio in the attic, and he wouldn't come down until
dinner. After I finished my homework and my mother
began to cook, I would unlatch the side passage door
silently and stand on the terrace, or if I was feeling brave,
go down the terrace steps to the pitch black lawn, wet

with dew, and look back at our tall, thin Victorian house, built from old maroon bricks.

Every other house on the street is short and suburban and semi-detached, but the bombs didn't happen to fall on our house during the war. When I was little, I thought a magic force field surrounded the house. Now I know it was chance. But at night, from the garden, the house did seem alive – the steamed-up glass in the kitchen door and the sink window shed warm yellow light onto the terrace and the sparkle and clatter of pans on the stove and plates in the sink sounded like a kind of talk. Two stories up the window of my father's studio always blazed white, as if the window itself were staring out into the dark garden.

That summer when I was twelve, my eldest sister Beatrice left home and went to live in Singapore with Dai Evans. She invited me to visit a few months later: weightless blue paper without any lines, almost transparent. At the end she wrote *we can pay your airfare*, underlined twice with three exclamation marks. My father refused. My middle sisters told me he disapproved of Dai. I sat on the steps in the side passage in my itchy red tights and red gingham dress and burned the letter with a blue plastic lighter.

The summer after that, Beatrice and Dai came back to visit. I was thirteen. They took me to a pub and we sat at one of the tables out the front, screened from the road by a trellis and pot plants. I had known Dai since my sister met him at Art school in London when I was nine or ten. Nothing was ever serious with him. That day I remember laughing so much that the sinews of my neck ached and I felt dizzy.

'Did you know Lydie, in Singapore, gum is illegal?' The way he said 'gum', with the practised, crisp consonants and the long vowel, was typical of his wonderful voice, so rich and comical. He sat beside my sister on the other side of the table, facing me. 'That's right, dear. Your sister was arrested recently.' He inhaled deeply on his cigarette, shook his head, raised his eyebrows and exhaled smoke. Then he leaned in confidentially, and his eyes narrowed to twinkling points. He smelt of foreign smells; whisky, tobacco, after shave lotion and some fascinating, rank maleness. 'Her offense? *Gum* possession. *Fay-wee sea-wee-arse*'.

'Don't listen to him, Lydia.' Beatrice said, but she was laughing too.

He grinned at her, the gleam in his eyes almost lost in the mass of tanned creases, like a metal scoop sunk in grain.

'The beaches are man-made. Artificial. Millions of cubic metres of sand, imported from Indonesia.' He drank from his glass. 'And it's so awfully hot. You'd hate it.'

When Beatrice went to the toilet he poured whisky in my diet coke from a silver flask and topped up his own glass. Then he looked out across the road. 'Do you know the rhyme that starts 'Yesterday, upon the stair'? Do they still teach silly things like that at school?' Behind the Lion Gates the park began to darken in the twilight. Nothing grew on the trellis and through the gaps I could see a ribbon of red brake lights, moving away. He wasn't talking to me anymore.

'Yesterday, upon the stair, I met a man who wasn't

there. He wasn't there again today, I wish, I wish, he'd go away.'

His voice was as rich as ever, but for once it didn't make me laugh. He said 'Here's to that', drank the contents of his glass and I think I knew even then that Dai didn't have all the answers.

Before they went back they gave me a conch shell from Borneo. I liked to curl all four of my fingers inside its sleek, salmon-pink chamber and hold it up like a flaky, horned fist. That winter I had a recurring dream that there was a crab alive inside it, and when I woke up in the dark for school it would have vanished from my bedside table. But it never did.

I used to imagine Beatrice and Dai walking by the sea's edge down some perfect white sand beach, Dai in khaki shorts and polo shirt, telling jokes, Beatrice in her air-blue summer dress and wide-brimmed straw hat, laughing, kicking the glaze of the receding sea at him. In my head it was Dai who found the shell in the turquoise shallows, and Beatrice who thought of giving it to me. They probably bought it from a hawker, or a souvenir shop at the airport.

∼

After the car was packed and I had showed them round first year halls, we went to sit in my tiny emptied room and I made them tea with my cheap white plastic kettle, which made cheap, plastic-tasting tea. My mother was perched awkwardly on my stripped mattress and my father sat in my desk chair, his dry, scaly hands clasped over his paunch. Without my possessions the furniture seemed cheap, tacky and transient, which it was. I looked at my cello case by the door and felt grateful that I wouldn't have to sit in the car with them, because of the concert that night.

'Where exactly is the library?' my father said throatily, as if he'd just woken up. 'I've seen dozens of morose carpeted hallways and several poky kitchens, but as of yet no library.'

My mother smiled at him in the way that she does: faintly amused, tolerant, bored. I suppose you could call it kind, but I wouldn't. She had shielded him from the brunt of their five children and allowed him to nourish his creative dreams because it made her stronger than him. Bdelloid rotifers lives in puddles and look like inverted commas driven by water-wheels. When the puddle dries they go to sleep and become unbreakable husks that can survive being boiled or frozen to absolute zero. She is something like that.

'Sorry, *Thomas*', I said, 'that this isn't *Aux*ford.'

'I'm quite aware of that, thank you.'

'And I'm quite aware of how disappointed you must be that I'm studying science at this second rate university.'

'That isn't true, Lydia.' He looked back at me mildly, with what I now realise was an appeal for conciliation and truce, rather than one of our battles. 'You still need books, don't you? Art and science haven't always been at odds, you know.'

My mother, sitting in the room's shadow at the other end of my bed, was examining her hands, as if they were someone else's. Maybe she would have told me about Beatrice then and there, but I've never been the sort of person who knows when to stop.

'Are you enjoying having Beatrice home? And her daughter, who none of us have even met, despite the fact she's six, because you hate Dai so much.'

My father shifted in the swivel chair. It creaked and moved a few inches.

'Let me guess – Olivia's in your bad books too, despite the fact she's six, because she cried, and interrupted your great artistic endeavours?'

My father stood up, looked at me with unforgettable reproach, and left the room.

The next afternoon was bright and warm and I felt apprehensive as I walked the familiar pavement from the train station, towards my parents' house. I could smell the blooms of the sweet bay magnolia that grew in Tom and Clara's front garden across the street, but the sour, decaying smell of old cut grass was stronger.

The front door was open that day, which was unusual, and the hall was cool and empty, but I could hear plates being washed in the kitchen and when I went in my sister Cressida was standing at the sink. She turned, smiled weakly and said 'welcome home', which was not how she normally talked. Usually she would say 'Oh, Lydia – could you pitch in to get dinner ready?' even if I hadn't seen her for months. She was always talking about pulling weight and pitching in. She looked thin

– the sinews in her neck stood out stridently as she examined me with her mother's fading green eyes. I asked her where everyone was and she began cleaning a teapot vigorously. 'Around,' she said, then added with satisfaction, 'Xanthe's not here yet.'

I went out onto the terrace, a cluttered nursery over-looking the rest of the garden, two steps down from the kitchen. Dozens of plastic pots were crowded together in clusters on one side, leaves fidgeting in the breeze. A plaster of Paris bird bath filled with soil rose from amongst them, brimming with pansies and geraniums. In a low wooden trough rosemary grew with the abundant vigour of a weed and a single muddy gardening glove lay beside a brand new pair of secateurs. They had been left unclipped and the clean, curved blades grinned in the bright sunlight. A figure slouched in my father's deckchair by the steps down to the lawn, facing the place where the cherry tree had once stood.

When I said 'hello, Dai', the body jolted and a face turned on me, unrecognisably sour and resentful for an instant. It made me jump, like a face in a dark window.

Then he stood up and smiled. He had developed a pot belly and his legs looked thin in his khaki shorts. When he put his arms around me I smelled the musky, old fashioned aftershave balm he had always used. He rested his palms on the points of my shoulders and looked at me, squinting, pursing his lips and shaking his head.

'What?' I was already smiling, the strangeness of the first impression rubbed away. 'What is it?

'The question is which, Lydie. Which?' He rested his forefinger and thumb on his chin. 'Let me think. The female scientist. Yes. You're either . . .' his mobile face became animated and young. Then the light in his eyes died and his face fell. 'No, you couldn't be. Could you?'

'I don't know what you're talking about!' I almost shouted it. He put his hands on his hips.

'So terribly quiet, serious, meticulous in the lab. And yet . . .' He gave me a grotesque, stagey wink. 'Outdrinks the rugby team? Extraordinary in bed?'

'I don't know what you're talking about.' I was embarrassed, and he must have seen it because he mumbled 'I won't believe it,' but then went towards the shed to assemble a second deck chair. He was shaky on his feet. We sat down, and I saw that he had cut himself shaving twice: once on his left cheek and again on the point of his chin, where a purple crust had formed.

'Did something happen here last night?'

He half-suppressed a yelp of laughter. 'Something, my dear, invariably does.'

A small, rickety table that had been left out in the weather stood in front of us; it looked vulnerable and I didn't recognise it. Upon it lay a pouch of rolling tobacco, a bottle cap serving as a tiny, temporary ashtray, and a heavy crystal tumbler I knew to be my father's, containing half an inch of whisky.

'Obviously everyone is upset about Bea. Your parents are, understandably.' His voice faltered. He rested his elbow on his knee and rubbed his face hard with his palm. 'You must be. I am.'

His head fell between his knees and I laid my arm across his collapsed shoulders. Beatrice had come home because she was ill; I knew that. But I only remember thinking that he was thirty-two, this man who had a child by my sister, and I was nineteen. I could not remember him ever saying anything serious.

'Let's have a drink', he said then, bracing upright suddenly. 'Let's just sit here and have a drink'. His fingertips encircled the brim of the tumbler; the table shivered on its spindly legs. He gripped the glass between his knees and fumbled at the cap of his silver hip flask.

I didn't want to watch him. I turned back to the house and saw my father rooted to the kitchen step, as if he had always been there. His plume of white hair moved absurdly in the breeze, but he was very pale and his fists were clenched at his sides.

'I want you to leave my house.' He spoke deliberately, as if the phrase had been turning over and over in his mind.

'I want you to leave tonight.'

Dai put the refilled glass on the table and stood up to face him, the deck chairs and me between them.

'Well, well,' he began theatrically, though I believe he was trying to sound serious and self-possessed. 'This is . . . what Bea wants, is it?'

As he spoke he tried to push the hip-flask and the tobacco pouch into the pockets of his shorts.

'I want it.'

'Clear as day!' Desperately he looked at me to share the joke. 'You know, your father might've made a first rate despot.' Then he looked down at the frail wooden table, and the crystal tumbler, and his voice became sinuous. 'I'll just pop in to see her, then.'

'My daughter is asleep and you won't disturb her. An

overnight bag has been packed for you. Collect the rest of your things tomorrow.'

Dai looked down at the crazy paving terrace below his feet. The design came from one of my father's abstract line drawings. His ownership of this old house, these bricks and walls, this lawn – it gave him weight. Now I understand that day was harder for my father, but then it just seemed terribly unjust, a mismatch. Dai picked up the tumbler, looked at it and said 'dreadful waste', then raised it towards my father. He said 'to your health' in a small, bitter voice and drank it off, then walked woozily towards the kitchen door. My father stepped soberly aside. I heard Cressida say something and Dai reply in his crisp voice, 'very kind of you Cressida, I must say, very decent indeed.' Then he was gone.

From the back seat of my parent's car, I watch her on the steps down from the front porch. My father plants a foot on the lowest step, ready to support her pale figure, prevent it from vanishing into the folds of her weightless white chemise. In his other hand he carries her patch-work bag, half-filled for this long weekend. Olivia dawdles on the top step, pointing at the wisteria that seems to fall from the sky. Martyred by opposing forces, Beatrice smiles – she does not think she can be seen, but I see her. It is a warm, joyous, resigned smile. When she sits next to me in the car I see that her shirt is not white but covered in a faint, washed out print of miniature giraffes. She smells of mouthwash.

Olivia falls asleep somewhere on the M4 corridor, head resting in Beatrice's sunken lap, feet rather higher on mine. I watch Beatrice's hairless forearm move as she collects the blonde curls of her daughter's hair and compresses them against her sleeping head. Over the roar of the engines and the air disappearing around us I ask her, *doesn't it make you angry?* I tell her that we have to *do* something about Dai, but she just wants to talk about the past.

'Do you remember when the cherry tree came down in the storm? You were about seven or eight – it was the September before I went to art school – and I was getting you ready, shoes and socks, in the kitchen. The storm had been so violent the previous night, and I'd hardly slept, but you were so good that morning. We couldn't find your shoes so I went up to look in your room and I saw the branches of the cherry tree fallen on the lawn out of your window, and then I saw you tear across the terrace and jump all three steps at once.'

I remember the feel of the dew through the soles of my tights and the grip of my mother's hand on my upper arm as she marched me back to the terrace. It is not a happy memory.

'Xanthe had taken Cressida down to the tree to pick cherries and their uniforms got muddy. She'd been smacked, she was angry, but it was nasty of her to trick you. And Mum shouldn't have smacked you. You suffered. It was unfair. But that's how it was.'

Beatrice looks at me. She has no eyebrows, just shadows where the follicles have died. 'It's strange, the way things happen. So many things need to fall into place to make things turn out as they do – and no-one can ever see all the pieces, or know how they will fall. We see the patterns of things afterwards, when we're told how to. At the time things just seem so cruel and ugly and random.'

I whisper, 'like Dad's paintings?' and she laughs. My mother turns around and smiles blandly at us.

'Lydia, you've always been so full-blooded. So literal.' Her voice dissolves in the thrust of petrol through the bodies of cars, the air always vanishing around us. 'Sometimes you need to let things run their course. We need to enjoy Wales.'

I say, 'fair enough. I understand.' Really I don't and I think she is giving up and I can't agree with her.

A fine drizzle is falling when we arrive. My father peers at the spidery, mildewed lock with unfamiliar keys in his hand. I have not been here in five years. The windows are coated in salt, and the slender walls are grubby cream pebbledash, except for a row of red bricks, two or three deep, exposed at the base of the building. All I can think is that the absurd little row of bricks is the saddest, most hilarious thing. Somebody planned this, invested some fragile, presumptuous hope in *this*. Did they think it would fool anyone? When the wind blows here the walls shake and the roof rattles like it's made of paper and glue.

I stand in the fine rain laden with a double duvet, which smells powerfully of home, and think of all the time I spent here alone with my parents. It was different for my brother and sisters, all here together. I drew Queens of England from post cards and wrote captions for them – mottoes, or answers they might give, if anyone cared to ask. I played my cello for my father in the warm orange light of the sitting room. He closed his eyes and between signatures I heard his deep, methodical breathing. A fire fizzed in the grate always; I watched it move as I played. My father was good at making fires.

And I listened to rain. I loved the heaviest, most torrential rain because you could not argue with it. In persistent rain you could hear tyres swishing through surface water on the B3626. I imagined the people in the car, gave them simple identities, listened to their conversations. When the rain is soft and drizzling like this, I close my eyes and let it fall on my face until it soaks my fringe and runs in droplets down my neck.

Across the dining-room from our large, half-occupied table, a couple sit by the window saying nothing to each other, only looking out of the large window at the old stone wall that divides the hotel garden from the plunging cliffs and the sea beyond. The wall has odd stones sticking out of its top layer, making it look like a set of broken teeth. The woman is not older than thirty and has greedily observed the unfilled places, the crying child and her pale, exhausted mother leaving the room. The man opposite her gazes wretchedly out of the window as if he wants to hurl himself out of it and over the old stone wall. Across the room are two tables of four, laid and ready. I hope that no-one else comes in.

My parents sit bolt upright like Victorian Puritans, watching the door for their two eldest children. It is 7 p.m. and my brother Marcus and his wife Marianne have still not arrived.

'Do you remember the big rounders match on the beach here, Cress?' Xanthe spreads butter thinly on a morsel of bread.

'I remember,' replies Cressida dutifully, empty seats either side of her.

'Even Dad played. I can't believe we used to swim naked in the sea. It's like ice.'

'I remember the drives back, with the vinegar smell of fish and chips.'

'Oh my god, and remember the tapes – the music tapes? Remember, Mum?'

'Yes.' She replies, looking sadly at the door. 'Marcus' pop music compilations.'

'Duran Duran! The Pet Shop Boys! We used to sing along.'

'You did.'

There is a pause. No-one is enjoying this.

'Shouldn't someone be helping Beatrice?' says my father at last, his voice trembling. 'Shouldn't someone be helping her?'

I stand up instinctively, but the dining room door opens and there is Dai, cradling a bottle of wine wrapped in pink tissue paper in the crook of his arm. His white roll neck jumper is too tight and exposes his pot belly. It looks as if it is oiled, and ought to be worn by an actual sailor. Staring at him, I forget that I am responsible for this and see him as my parents do – an absurd, unwanted intruder.

'I'm – sorry,' he mumbles at last. 'It's not . . .' He does not finish his sentence.

I follow him out of the room. In the hall, Beatrice faces us.

'Hello Beatrice,' he says. 'Where's Olivia?'

'Why are you here?' Her voice is hoarse and low. It rattles in her chest.

'I – well, I spoke to *Lydie*, as you know, and we thought . . .' I wince at Lydie. It sounds so artificial. He looks at the carpet beneath his feet. 'I shouldn't have come.' On the wall behind Beatrice is a painting I recognise. The scene is familiar – scudding clouds in a pale blue sky, cold-looking sand scattered with dark rocks, a forked stream heading for the sea. Grim, soaring cliffs. There is nothing special about it, no motion or life. The price tag reads £1400. I wonder how long it has been on the wall, and whether the artist still thinks about it.

I turn to go but Beatrice says 'you stay there.' Then she looks at Dai.

'You shouldn't have drunk so much, so often. You shouldn't have forgotten Olivia's fifth birthday. You should not have brought your boys back to our home. To our bed. And you should not have goaded my father as you did, or come here. Yet you did all of these things.'

Dai's chin drops to his sternum. A faint nasal sound expires in a gasp and he says 'Quite right, quite right', raising his eyes for a second with evident effort. The bottle of wine shakes by his side. 'I'm a monster. But I love you, Beatrice. Always have. Always will.'

'I know.' Beatrice looks beyond him as if at an unremarkable view from a garden window. Her voice is calm. 'It makes things worse.'

≈

Beatrice died on 5 September, five weeks after the meal. The weekend of the funeral was hot, and everyone was on the roads trying to get to the parks, to sit outside together and read the papers and drink wine from plastic cups and make the most of what would most likely be the last of the sun.

Dai wore a creased, ill-fitting white linen suit with a lime green silk shirt and a red woven 1970s tie that was square-cut at the bottom, and which my brother Marcus had to do up properly for him before the service began. I almost laughed when I saw him. Olivia sat on my mother's lap during the service in her pretty sky-blue dress and little felt hat. I remember the sound of gravel crunching as we walked away from the service towards the cars and the sight of my mother walking behind with Dai, her arm round his lower back, her eyes fixed straight ahead as he twisted his head back towards the cemetery and buried his face in her shoulder. I believe that she was holding him up, that she stopped him from falling down.

I remember sitting next to my father for the service, and he put his arm around me and held my head to his heaving chest. I remember that he stroked my hair.

Grief is stronger than any principles, but it doesn't change them.

≈

I had been standing next to him facing her stone for a long time, saying nothing, staring at the white orchid flowers we had brought. Some bouquets were two weeks old and had started to wither, but it was too early to move them.

'We fly back to Singapore in two weeks.' He was still looking at the grave stone. 'Olivia needs to start senior school. Extraordinary.' He tried to laugh.

I knew that Olivia's dependence on him would not change his ways. I looked at his tanned, clean shaven jaw and the flecks of grey in his hair. He was a capricious, ego-centric alcoholic, hedonistic, even depraved. But he was soft, too, and sentimental and indulgent in a way that daughters need their fathers to be sometimes, and that all too often they aren't.

$\sim$

That September my parents sat together on the terrace drinking gin and tonics, looking across the lawn to the place where the cherry tree used to be. My father paid less attention to the lawn and it grew long, and thick with weeds.

I read some of the books and journal articles on the second year reading list and played with Olivia, who stayed with us for those two weeks while Dai went to Bristol to arrange the sale of the flat he owned there. She had a miniature fold-up pushchair, two plastic dinosaurs and a toy dog attached to a rigid stick that served as a lead. She called it Snowy, although it was pink. She would strap the dinosaurs – a triceratops and a diplodocus – into the pushchair with such care, and speak to them so softly.

'Now then my dear, you have to be good, my darling. Or mummy will be very angry, you know.'

And then she would push her pushchair around the lawn and drag Snowy behind her, his nose bumping along the lawn. One day I asked her where she was going.

'To the doctors.'

'Where is the doctors?

She stopped and looked through me, not pointing, not making any sign. 'The doctors is here.'

One afternoon I heard my mother tell Olivia that her mother was dead and wasn't coming back to collect her, and of course she should be sad, but that it wasn't her fault in any way, and all would be well, and she would grow up to be a beautiful, intelligent woman, just like her mother.

I told her that her mother was in the rain. One dark day towards October when the wind had started to rattle the windows and threaten rain, I told her that whenever it rained she should listen for her mother's voice: when the rain was heavy, her mother was laughing – or crying, or shouting, which everyone must some times – though it cannot last for long and will always level out into the middling rain that was her mother's presence, not happy, or sad, or angry but just present, soaking into the roots of plants and trees, falling onto green leaves like a fine, cooling mist. I told her there would be dry spells when no rain fell, which would be hard for plants, when they would have to rely on the deeper stores of water in the earth. But the rain would always come back – hammering on the roof some dark night, or tapping on the windowsill in the half-light morning, asking to be let in.

MATTHEW MORGAN

ABSENT STARS

TOM CLIMBS DOWN the ladder; the auteur films from the top. The ladder is blotted to the wall and aims down a narrow passage. Looking up, Tom can see that the manhole cover is perched to allow only a slice of light through, he squints to make out the auteur. He knows the auteur can't see him though; past a certain point, all you can is darkness from up there. The auteur joins Tom at the base. They walk through a number of dusty corridors before emerging in part of the old subway's tunnel. Tom turns the torch off and they begin making their way home in darkness.

Tom and the auteur had been above ground to get food and clothes, while keeping a look out for whatever else that could be of use, a piece of furniture or a gas canister for cooking. It'd been busy up there: people, cars, the warm bustle of the city, the loose threads of sound that merely flirt with the ear, sirens, music, laughter. Tom often tempts himself with thoughts of staying up there, returning to his family, his wife, his son. Every time the atmosphere of the city inspires a feeling of nostalgia, every time the same friction in his heart, a childlike longing.

A group of rats pass by their feet, barely distinguishable and seemingly as one animal, more like a glitch in the darkness of the tunnel's floor. The subway's track has gone, they salvaged and sold what had been left behind long ago: *we ate good that week*. The tunnel's arc can only really be sensed, it feels more like the darkness is insidiously lurching over you.

Everything is still and quiet in the tunnel, there is a sense of timelessness, you could be walking on the spot and never know it. Like many things down here, walking through the tunnel for Tom has become an unconscious act, more a feeling or a mood than an action. Tom looks to the auteur, he's a mere notion in the darkness, a stencilled outline against the relentless black. The auteur seems intrigued by the dark. He always films this walk, filming the sounds more than anything else, their breathing and the scuffle of loose stones beneath their feet that almost find the rhythm of music.

Tom is thirty five years old and has been living down here, in New York's old subway, for two years now. Others have been down here longer, some less. John has been down here fifteen years. The girl, not even a year. About four months ago, the auteur had said that he wanted to film them and their lives and offered them some money for the privilege. Tom said sure but told him to keep the money, and that it would be fine if he could just help out now and again. The auteur has been sleeping on the kitchen floor during his stay; he didn't bring anything with him other than the camera.

The camp emerges to their right as they follow the tunnel's bend. A couple of small fires are alight. The light gives the darkness a shape, a kind of body that it doesn't have in pitch black form. The camp consists of seven houses. The houses are more like huts than buildings per se, they're cramped and rudimentary. Most of the homes are made from pallets and random bits of scaffolding with fabric pulled taut across them, some people have used mattresses as walls, one person has used part of a child's climbing frame and so has a slide sticking out of the wall like a dissenting tongue. Fifteen year old veteran, John, has three sides brick and mortar. Tom's is one room, his mattress and sofa on one side and separated using a large piece of cloth from his kitchen that is on the other. The kitchen is mainly cupboards; most of the cooking is done outside on the gas powered hob or over a fire.

The girl lives in a sort of tent adjacent to Tom's house. Her name is Amber, Tom doesn't think this is her real name, at least not the one her mother gave her. He thinks the name is probably some attempt at escape, at reinvention. She is nine or ten. She's a runaway. Her story comes out at random times. My mum used to hit me, she'll say as they sit next to a fire cooking food. She is always dirty and yet pretty. She has two floral dresses that she interchanges between; Tom washes these for her and always keeps an eye out for shoes or clothes whenever he goes up to the surface. He tries to take care of her as much as he can but she is reluctant and weary of him. She has an intelligence and level of suspicion that is beyond her years; Tom finds something admirable and yet sad about this.

Amber is often wandering about by herself and whenever she goes off, the auteur will wait for her to reach a certain distance before he starts filming her. Tom thinks he must have countless shots of her walking away from the camp, her image slowly fading and swallowed by the darkness and disappearing before the tunnel's bend. It's unclear if he is searching for something new each time he films this or whether there is something important crucial or addictive found in the repetition.

'My mum used to cry after she hit me, it was like an angry crying, like she was angry at herself. After the first time she hit me, I stood in the doorway and she was sat on the floor of her room, crying, and I told her I was sorry. I was sorry without really knowing why.'

Tom is trying to fix one of the walls as the rats that have tried to burrow underneath have created a hole and dislodged part of the wall. He shovels some soil into the hole, the ground down here is mostly arid dirt and stones. The auteur pours in some water to help toughen up the soil and give it an adhesive quality. They rely on the light from a nearby fire to see what they're doing. Tom tests the wall's wooden panel, he tries to rock it back and forth, it doesn't move. 'Better,' he says. As Tom is putting the shovel away, he notices the auteur filming the water as it's absorbed by the ground.

∾

Tom doesn't ask how the films going, they never talk
about the film, it's like it both is and isn't a thing between
them, he doesn't know if this makes it something incon-
sequential or something severe, but they don't talk about
it. If they talked about it, Tom feels that some frequency or
pitch would be unnecessarily disturbed, some unspoken
agreement that is essential to their relationship and the
repose that exists between them.

A man in the distance is struggling with a trolley that's
filled with plastic bags. Tom and the auteur watch him as
he enters the camp. The auteur raises the camera to his
right eye and starts filming.

'He keeps dying plants,' Tom says. 'He takes plants
from up there and replants them down here and they die,
maybe one or two days you can still look at their beauty
but then they close in on themselves and die. He calls
them his children, he watches over them but he doesn't
water or care for them, I don't know why, I'm not sure if
he knows why, maybe it's like you said a while ago about
things that can't be communicated, I don't know. Maybe
he sees them as beautiful still or maybe he likes watching them die, it doesn't seem like he takes any pleasure
in it though. I've watched him standing over them and he
seems basically absent, it's strange, it's like he is there
and not there, watching over the plants.'

'And they're dying.'

'They're dying. They close in on themselves, they
shrivel up and bend over, their petals break off. I used to

go over and look at them but now I can't. I don't know why but I just can't look at them anymore.'

'One or two days of beauty.'

'One or two days of beauty.'

Tom and the auteur are sat around a fire on an old car seat and a leather reading chair that has no legs. They're eating the spaghetti Bolognese Tom has made, one of the better meals they've had recently.

Amber returns just as they are finishing. 'Hey, saved some food for you if you're hungry,' Tom says. She picks up the plate of food, smiles at Tom and sits on the floor and begins eating using her hands. Tom goes to pass her a fork but she waves it away. Her hair looks cartoonishly styled, frizzy and matted. Her face is as dirty as ever, which accentuates her brown eyes. She eats in the same ardent way that everyone seems to eat down here.

She looks at the fire as she eats, eyes narrowed to a point of scrutiny as if she's trying to decipher something from the ebullient shifts of orange and yellow. The auteur has left his chair; Tom looks over his shoulder and notices him filming her from afar.

'I drank a lot.'

'What?'

'I used to drink a lot.'

'Tom, you don't have to tell me this.'

'No, it's fine, I want to tell you this, I don't why. But yeah, I used to drink a lot and I don't . . . maybe I couldn't handle what I had, a family, a wife and a kid, but my drinking became more intense around the time my son was born, I think it was fear looking back, or that I had to like destroy something I had fear of losing, that probably doesn't make any sense but if you have something that you don't want to lose sometimes you destroy it before somebody can take it away from you. I think I can almost cope with destroying something instead of losing it or having someone take it away from me.'

'Do you miss your family?'

'Yes, every day.'

John lives at the far end of the camp, he's a big jovial man with an almost overwhelming kindness. His story is vague. Tom heard that he murdered someone and fled fifteen years ago, others say he was a millionaire but lost it all to criminals and was driven underground when they came to take more than his business. It doesn't matter either way to Tom, he likes the fact that a man like John, who could easily be harmful, chooses to be kind. For the Christmases that Tom has been here, John has dressed up as Santa Clause each time. His Santa Clause act is layered in the pathos and self-consciousness that their situation warrants, it lightens the mood and allows them all to laugh at themselves, if only briefly.

John has three dogs, one of them is blind, he acquired them all during Tom's time down here and Tom has seen firsthand how John has trained and improved them from the skinny and feral animals they were into the relatively disciplined and well fed animals they are now. Tom is leaning on the pen that John has built for his dogs.

'They get fed better than we do down here those dogs,' Tom says. John laughs, this is a common joke that they share, it's lost its humorous bite but the familiarity is warm and comforting.

'I think one of them might be ill, keeping my eye on her,' John says.

'Yeah. Which one?'

'Poppy,' John says, referring to the blind one.

'Man, poor girl, can't catch a break.'

'Tell me about it.'

'What you gonna do?'

'I dunno, my vet, you know my guy up there, well, he's moving away so I'm gonna try and get him to take a look at her before he goes, but I dunno if I'll be able to afford any treatment or operation or anything if it's bad news.'

'Man.'

'Yeah.'

Tom stands under the dripping pipe and rubs soap on his naked body, he's only partially hidden by a wooden screen. He feels the auteur filming him but he doesn't mind. The shower's base is cold and dirty, the slightly raised design on its surface allows the dirt to form into brown veins, a slimy texture moves against the bottom of his feet as if alive. Usually the shower is a steady stream but sometimes it comes down in jolts and lumps of water as if the pipe is vomiting. The water is always cold, more punitive than refreshing. He thinks about his son and the questions he must have, questions that go unanswered.

One of Tom's neighbours, Stef, is telling him about an article on the auteur – who she calls the mad director – she'd read recently. She says how after reading it she thinks that the auteur is as fucked up as everyone else down here, that the article had said how he's considered a genius, that he turned down prizes and awards in his heyday but that he hasn't made a film for ten years, that the industry is wondering where he is, that rumours are circulating that he's gone underground, literally, into New York's old subway system to live with the vagrants, that he's lost all his money, gone mad and moved down there. She says that the article mentioned nothing about a film or anything but it had the last known photograph of the mad director and it was from ten years ago and that it was definitely him, it said he was now forty years old but how she thinks he looks a lot older than that.

'Told you.'

'Yeah, they're dying. I thought you said you couldn't look at these anymore.'

'Yeah, well.'

The flowers are bent over and closed in on themselves like things waiting to be forgiven.

John's dogs can be heard playing with a new squeaky toy, its squeals for mercy rising above the pop and snap of a fire that sits near. Tom and the auteur are sat outside his home, leaning back on their chairs as if basking in the night's sky, but really they are staring into the tunnel's ceiling, an inexorable night that is absent stars. They begin joking about things they can see, a familiar game. They invent constellations and the path of a comet; they debate on the destinations of planes and the type of birds that migrate at night. They stop the game before it passes from a joke and into longing.

'Why do you film her from afar?' Tom asks.

'I see something in the girl.'

'What do you see?'

'What you see.'

'I don't see anything, I just don't want her to get hurt.'

'So you see something to protect.'

'Yeah, I guess.'

The auteur is opening up about the film. He's talking about how he is filming it in black and white. How he is going to use a technique on the film itself that provides it with a slight blemish, kind of like a self-inflicted wound. The auteur's intention is that the blemish won't be obvious but will imbed itself into the audience's subconscious, at least he hopes. He says how the audience will be provided with an uneasy sensation, a feeling that something is wrong with the film outside of just what they are seeing, it will be something that stalks the edge of their consciousness, they will be disturbed by something but they won't know why or what. He wants to put something right in front of them but just out of their grasp, a preoccupation that they can't solve and can't really talk about, he wants to provoke something in them, a frustration, a kind of madness of the soul, he says.

Amber sometimes goes for walks through the vast and anonymous tunnels adjacent to the one their camp resides in. Be careful, Tom always says when he sees her going off, and she'll shoot him an ironic smile in return. Tom knows the dangers of the tunnels, there are the obvious dangers: vagrants, animals, sharp and contemptuous debris but there are also the more penetrating dangers, the dangers of your own mind – the darkness serves as a blank canvas on to which the mind paints its own hell. Memories – with a retinue of hopes, dreams and longings – come out of the dark with the speed and skill and precision of a ringmaster's whip.

He wonders why she goes, what she sees and what she feels. Maybe her walks are motivated not by a sense of escape but discovery. Maybe she feels that if she goes further into the darkness she can find some core truth, some meaning, mundane or emphatic it doesn't matter, just something that is akin to understanding, something that is like her, and maybe this is how she sees the dark, not as different from herself but *of* herself, and to walk into it, exposed and vulnerable, is to open herself up to herself. For her, the dark is reflective as opposed to opaque, and she is willing to risk consumption for some measure of understanding no matter how tenuous or banal.

'Why haven't you made a film for ten years?'
    'I don't know, time isn't a concern to me.'
    'But ten years.'
    'You read the article?'
    'No, but you hear things down here.'

One of John's dogs does this sort of wail, sometimes. It's like a sad siren. It's loud but has the kind of politeness that comes with the terse and careful speech at a funereal, an adopted measure of grief. It's obvious the dog is in pain when it's doing this, not ostensible pain but probably something within and only known to itself, the sort of pain that defines the essence of a thing and makes it act in ways that it doesn't understand.

Tom opens the door to the hut that he calls a toilet. A bucket sits below an old wooden chair, which has a hole bored through it. He looks at the bucket long enough to see that it is full before gripping the handle that has a moisture he tries not to think about. The shit and piss sloshes with a grim vibrancy as he carries the bucket to the drain where all the camp's waste is taken. He fights the noise as well as the smell. He bends down alongside the bucket to pour the contents away. As the lurid mixture passes through the drain's bars an unsettling warmth and vapour is accompanied by putrid smells that flick and writhe underneath his nose, causing him to close his eyes. Using the edge of the bucket he pushes wayward bits of shit between the bars. Who knows where it all goes. He returns to the camp and washes the bucket out and places it back into the hut to begin the cycle all over again.

'She used to come into my room late at night, after she'd been out drinking or doing whatever, and she'd lie on my bed with me when I was pretending to be asleep and she'd tell me that she loved me. She was always fucked up when she did this, she'd drool and slur, I could taste her breath in my mouth and I could smell her perfume and the smell of cigarettes. Then the man she'd brought back for that night would usually shout from the other room asking her what she was doing, he sounded drunk too, then she'd kiss me on the cheek, a goodbye sort of a kiss, and call me her little girl and go to the man.'

'The melancholia of things completed.'

'What?'

'In answer to your question the other day about me not finishing a film for ten years. The melancholia of things completed. Nietzsche said it, I think. There's a certain sadness in things fulfilled, as if meaning is pulled away when something is finished as opposed to its completion giving meaning. I have a feeling of loss when I finish something instead of a feeling of having created something.'

The auteur is filming from a distance. Tom can see him, filming from the opposite side, looking as if he's wearing the tunnel's darkness as a cloak, a pallid glow to his hands and face. The man plants the flowers in the arid soil with the conspicuous lack of passion normally reserved for a chore. He holds the flowers as if he is strangling a neck and pushes them into the ground, it's as if they are resisting, being forced into the ground against their will.

Tom and the auteur have been to the surface and are walking back into the camp. There is a crowd of people, some Tom recognises some he doesn't, around John's dog pen. One person is threatening John, someone is asking him why, someone is asking him how, more accusations than questions. John is shaking, his face is red and has the oily patina of tears. Two of John's dogs are loose and wandering around the camp, they look lost and forlorn.

The man who owns the dying plants is sat with his back to the pen, he's rambling to no one in particular, he is saying how he got here too late, he heard screams, he says, got here too late, he keeps saying he heard screams, his speech devolves into these few words: screams, too late. Another man says that he got the dog, killed it, he had no choice, he got the dog with the shovel, he says this without any suggestion of pride.

When the crowd notice Tom the arguing stops, everyone turns to face him. The crowd part slightly and allow Tom through. A kind of dignity and pity exists between the crowd and Tom, a moment where words are no longer appropriate or needed. He looks in the pen and sees the dead dog, then he sees her body, her floral dress torn, her hair splayed across her face in the way only a struggle could produce, her limbs are crooked and still, the blood on the floor is like a bruise on dark skin. He falls to his knees, he tastes dirt for only a second before there is darkness and the sound of people as if heard from underwater.

After he wakes he goes over to a bowl of water and washes his face, seeking support in the routine as much as anything else. He sits on the leather reading chair. He wishes he could stop his thoughts, the crazed syntax of regret that is running through his mind, the brawl of his emotions. The fires around him emanate a mournful glow, their flames nothing more than whispers of light. He stares at the stark inadequacy of his clenched fists. His mouth quivers with the prospect of apology. He feels the strange recklessness of grief: he no longer cares, to the point where he thinks he could plough his hand into a fire's embers, shovel them down his throat and it wouldn't matter.

He knows that when his mind is at its most vulnerable and porous she will be there – images of her that are burned into the lens of his consciousness, vibrant and fresh and yet excruciatingly distant.

He thinks about his family.

He gets up and walks towards the tunnel's darkness, passing the camera that has been left at the entrance, its case split open, the fragile images captured on its film now exposed, coiled and strewn: ruined, but still carrying an element of beauty.

DAN POWELL

STORM IN A TEACUP

THE CUP IS Alice Stout's. It is a simple off-white thing, one of many to be found in the café she runs with husband Sid. From outside comes the rumble of Bridgenorth's cliff railway, heralding the imminent arrival of the morning trade. But right now, it is not quite opening time for The Tea Cosy and Alice sits at one of the tables she has already laid. She gulps her tea, then stops still for just a moment or two, her elbows on the table, her hands wrapped around the cup. It is empty but for a thin layer of sweet milky tea coating the ceramic inside. This is how the storm begins, as if somehow the heat from Alice's hands warms the cup and, by conduction, the air inside.

It is important to note that there is nothing unusual about the cup itself. Today, this sunny morning in 1973, it is what is about to happen inside the cup that is unusual. A centre of low pressure surrounded by a system of high pressure is about to develop, which will result, when the opposing forces meet, in the creation of winds and storm clouds. Cumulonimbus. Literally, accumulated rain.

Even if the slowly emerging systems of the storm were visible, Alice would not see them. Her head is filled with 1951, specifically the summer of that year. In her pocket she has seven torn ticket stubs for the cliff railway. She has kept them, tucked away in the bottom of her jewellery box, for decades. She has not thought of them in years, yet this morning she woke and simply had to find them, tuck them safely into the pocket of her apron, bring them with her when she came down from the flat. Thoughts of the tickets crowd Alice's head while her hands inexplicably warm the cup she holds before her like a chalice.

The rumble from the cliff railway grows louder and shakes Alice from her thoughts. She crosses the café and places the cup down on the serving counter next to the till. Inside the air churns and swirls. Differing pressures prepare to meet as Alice gets on with laying the tables.

In the crumpled row of buildings leading to the cliff railway in High Town, the Tea Cosy huddles between a dusty antique emporium and the grease-smeared shop-front of the local fish and chip shop. A faded sign swings above the door, the ghost of a painting. A teapot upon a tray, surrounded by cups and saucers, a milk jug and sugar bowl. The teapot in the picture wears what must once have been a colourful cosy, now grayed and faded; its yellows turned to mustard, its blues shifting to smoke, its reds barely pink, more the muddy brown of old tea stains. A sallow net curtain hangs in the window through which little can be seen from the outside.

Sid Stout, Alice's husband of just over twenty-five years if you count the summer of 1951, or just under if you don't, stands in the kitchen looking out through the hatch, watching Alice lay the café's seven circular tables. She looks good for her age. A much younger woman would be proud of the fall of her red hair and the way she fills her simple red dress and striped apron. It is her eyes that Sid is watching for though. Her eyes are green. He struggles for the right word. Emerald? Apple? Forest? He settles for sage, both the shade and the peppery flavour seem right for Alice. It strikes Sid that though the café they share is worn about the edges and, by his own admission, he himself is frayed with age, Alice still glows. But even as he takes pleasure at the way she moves about the room, the sense of unease, with him since he woke this morning, grows. This feeling, that he has forgotten something important, looms over him.

'What are you looking so glum for?' Alice asks. She is stood at the door to the café, about to open up and looks back at him with an exasperation that they both know is also love.

'Nothing.'

'Still love me?' she says and Sid does not hesitate with his reply.

'Always.'

She smiles. 'Good. Now get back to work.'

And with that, Alice flips the sign hanging in the window from CLOSED to OPEN.

Miniature hot air currents climb the curve of the cup's tea stained surface, cool air down drafts in the centre of the tiny space. It is still too soon to tell what form this particular storm will take, if there will be hail or thunder and lightning, whether it will be a rainstorm, a snowstorm, an ice storm, a tropical storm, or a hurricane, if it will cause flooding or wildfires. Forgotten by Alice as she darts back and forth from kitchen to café, unnoticed by Sid as he stirs and chops and warms oil in the kitchen, the cup sits on the faded Formica beside the till, the storm inside growing.

Tommy sits at his usual table, having scraped together enough coppers for a full English. It will be his last visit of the week to the Cosy as payday is still three days away. He smokes a roll-up. The twine holding his trousers in place and fastening his jacket about him marks Tommy as a man in need of a wife. A pair of yarks band his knees, holding his trouser cuffs clear of the dried mud upon his work boots. His hat, a worn cap with a well-thumbed peak, sits on the table along with his tobacco pouch and Rizlas.

Tommy is the only customer to have walked the cliff steps this morning, the funicular rail cars passing him at least twice as he clambered up the steep stone path. It was a choice between a ticket or breakfast and when Alice brings out his eggs and bacon he digs in, a grin bursting through his furiously bristling beard.

'Cheers, Alice,' he says.

'You're very welcome, Tommy love,' she replies, already walking away.

A fine woman, a real catch that one. Tommy smiles, imagining what it must be like to have such a woman for a wife. Egg yolk runs into the thatch of his beard and he wipes it away with a threadbare cuff. Tommy sees Sid watching from the kitchen hatch, unsure if he is looking at Alice or at Tommy himself. He reddens but no one notices, his flushed cheeks too well hidden under his thick beard. The only visible sign of his embarrassment is the sweat breaking on his forehead but everyone knows Tommy walks the cliff steps each morning, reason enough for anyone to be sweating cobs.

Emily Blakemore sits at the table nearest the window, her terrier, Clarence, snuffling at her feet. Every now and then she twitches the smoke-yellowed net curtain up and scans the cobbles leading down to the cliff railway.

'He'll be along in a minute,' Alice says.

Emily drops the curtain as if stung. She hides her eyes by fixing them on the menu card and catches her breath.

'Tea and a crumpet?' Alice says.

The bell above the door jangles. The man entering wears a suit and overcoat and his polished brogues snap on the worn linoleum. He crosses the café without a word

and takes a seat at the table furthest from the other customers, his back to them.

'Tea and a crumpet, ta.'

As Emily say this, her eyes are locked on the shoulders of the man across the room, her bosom heaving
beneath her dress. Alice nods and slips across to the
smartly dressed man. Emily smiles as he orders tea and
a crumpet.

Clarence is the first to sense the developing storm, his
ears leaping forward, furrowing the fur of his brow. The
dog flicks his eyes this way, that way, their frantic movement emphasised in the stillness of his body. He hears a
crumpling sound and turns to face it but cannot see inside
the cup from where he is on the floor. The little dog looks
to his owner but Emily's eyes remain fixed on the back
and shoulders of the suited man. The crumpling sound
comes again, louder. It drags Clarence up on his paws,
sends him scampering back and forth under the table.

'Clarence!' Emily barks at the dog and, obediently, he
collapses back to the floor, his head on his paws. He hears
the crumpling sound again and rolls his eyes once more
up to his mistress, but she is watching the man again.
Clarence stares dolefully at the ankles of the others but
they are all too busy with their food or their paper or each
other. Clarence drops his eyes and whines.

The bell above the door rings again and a lad in jeans and a donkey jacket steps in. His face is straggled with long hair and a largely failed attempt at a beard. He sits at the table between Emily and the suited man, causing Emily to sigh. Her huffing has the lad, David, look to his left and right for the cause of the offence she is so obviously taking, but seeing nothing of note he collapses back in the chair.

'Coffee,' he says to Alice once she makes her way to him. 'Please.'

He has been awake much of the night, finally sleeping on a bench facing out over the sandstone cliffs, the rush of the Severn, one hundred feet below, reduced to an ambient lullaby. The rattle and hum of the funicular railway's first departure from High Town woke him. Before rising from the dew-damp bench he sat, the river and Low Town before him, the cliff railway rattling along beside him, the castle ruins still sleeping behind him, and he watched the cliff rail cars leave and arrive, leave and arrive. Now, in the warm of the café, he watches Alice take in his disheveled appearance.

'I can pay,' he says, pulling a handful of coins from his pocket.

'No love, don't fret about that.' Alice smiles and points to the rear of the shop. 'You can use the basin out back to clean yourself up while I get your coffee.'

David nods, thanks her and scuffs across the café and out the back.

'Oi,' shouts Sid as the young lad passes.

'Leave 'im be,' Alice calls through the kitchen hatch.

'Not another waif and stray,' Sid mutters loud enough

for Alice to hear, then he smiles. 'You're a soft one Alice Stout,' he says.

'Must be to stay married to you,' she calls back, and right then her thoughts turn to the ticket stubs in her pocket. Something must show in her eyes because Sid stops sharp and, feeling suddenly tense but unable to say why, watches after her as she turns to see to the boy's coffee.

∼

Cyril, sat at the table nearest the kitchen, sips his tea. Between every other sip he checks the time on his wrist-watch as if the act of his drinking were somehow part of the device's workings. A newspaper rests on the table before him. He glances at the open pages, running his hand through his receding, close-cropped hair. He checks his watch again, this time holding it up to his ear, search-ing for the tick and tock and tick of it. Satisfied that time is moving as it should be he half turns. Somewhere in the corner of his vision he is aware of someone watching him and swings his head the other way to better take in whoever it is.

His eyes lock upon the woman with the dog at the table nearest the café window. He recognises her from the library. They have spoken once or twice as she stamped his books but he only knows her by her surname. She stares across at him and he back at her and he grows sud-denly clammy. Feeling his face flush, he yanks a hand-kerchief from his breast pocket, covers both palms with the white cotton and sweeps it over his face and up to his diminished hairline. The upward action leaves what little remains of his fringe sticking up like a poorly pruned bush. Folding the sweat-damp handkerchief he glances across once more to find her still looking and turns hurriedly back to his tea. He takes a sip, checks his watch, takes another sip. When he turns in his seat once more, the scruffy boy is back at his table and lean as he might Cyril's view is blocked.

A supercell thunderstorm is characterized by the presence of a deep rotating updraft or mesocyclone forming as strong changes of wind speed and/or direction sets part of the lower atmosphere spinning in invisible, tube-like rolls. Supercells are often isolated from other rain-storms and, most importantly, can be any size. The one forming in the cup is picking up speed. The first rumbles of its churning clouds are too quiet for any but Clarence to hear. The cup sits where it has been left, the magnificent event taking place inside it unnoticed by the Cosy's proprietors and patrons alike. The storm clouds brew and swirl like malignant cappuccino froth.

Outside the Tea Cosy a blue sky promises much for the day. A few shapes hurry past the window, folk on their way to wherever, lacking the time for a cup of tea or a need for breakfast, oblivious to the extraordinary nature of what is about to happen inside.

The coffee is bitter and makes David wince with each sip, but the heat of it begins to revive his spirits. He wraps his fingers round the cup, warming his hands along with his insides. Looking up he sees the waitress looking over. She smiles and he smiles back, mouthing a thank you for the use of the washstand as much as the coffee.

Placing his cup down upon its saucer he checks his pocket. The jingle of coins is reassuring and he does not feel the need to count them. The weight and sound are heavy enough to assure him he has the cash to pay for his drink, a ride to Low Town on the cliff railway and a bus to work from the stop below.

Perhaps he will try Liz from the phone box on the way, if he can think of what to say. Sipping once more at his coffee, fingers wrapped once more around the cup, he mulls over how to fix things with a girl who no longer loves him.

Everyone for the moment served, Alice steps back into the kitchen and walks to where Sid stands washing up, his back to her. She steps close in to him, slipping her arms under his, wrapping them about his chest. She rests her head for a moment on his back at the place where his neck and shoulders meet. Her hands slide inside his shirt and rest between the fabric of his vest and shirt as if between bedsheets. He turns his head toward her and she tips her toes and lifts her lips to meet his cheek. Sid smiles, a fag balanced between his lips.

'What's that for?'

'For being here.'

Something they always say.

Her head fills with thoughts of the tickets and what they mean. His head dizzies with another rush of unease. Sid turns his face back to the soapy water of the sink and Alice slips from him like she's stepping out of a dress. At that exact moment a shriek fills the near silence of the café.

≈

Everyone is on their feet and looking at the counter. Light flashes and cracks from within the teacup. It trembles imperceptibly with the tiny power of the storm inside. Emily shrieks again. Clarence yaps at her feet then begins to stalk toward the storm-filled tea cup, his growls an unending curl of consonants. The storm cloud answers with a rumble that sends the terrier skittering back to the feet of his owner, yelping.

'How is it the cup ain't moving?' Sid leans in, staring hard at the churning thunderhead. He purses his lips then blows a blast of air at the cup and the cloud ruffles, spiraling with the updraft from within. Sid, growing more obfuscated as the clouds darken, raises a hand to the cup.

'Sid, what're you doing?'

'Calm down, Alice love. Just gonna give it a little poke.'

Pointing a tobacco-stained finger at the dense cauliflower blossoms of cloud, he inches it forward, hesitates, then dabs it in. A flash and crack echoes on the walls of the café.

'Bleedin' hell,' he bellows and whips his finger out. The

end is black and smoking and he blows on it for a second or two before plunging it into his mouth.

'Sid, language.'

'Hmmmit bleeeebiin yuuurts,' Sid groans through the finger clenched in his cheek.

They have made a horseshoe around the cup, all except for Clarence who lays whining beneath a table. Cyril squats, his eyes level with the cup, watching intently. 'There,' he says, 'see that?'

A tiny flash, like the spark of a flint lighter, illuminates the cloud from beneath. A roll of thunder follows, a sound like fingers tapping on a table top.

'A proper storm then, lightning and everything,' Cyril says, a surprised chuckle shaking him for a second. 'Remarkable.'

No one speaks for a time, mesmerised by the adumbrating swirl of air. They lean in as one, lulled to silence and stillness by the tiny ferocity of the wind escaping the cup and, together, they begin to see.

For Alice it is her love for Sid she sees twisting itself inside and out, a dense cloud of emotion that rolls and thunders. It is the love that had her say nothing when she found, all those years ago, Sid had been 'taking tea' with Reeny Moseley from Low Town. He was seen and word got back to Alice but she never spoke of it. Before the gossip found its way to her ear, she knew he'd been up to something because she found the ripped ticket stubs for the cliff railway in the pocket of his trousers. Always one ticket. Not the two half stubs still joined she put in her purse as they made their way home from The Black Boy Inn down on the Cartway on a Friday night. Love held her tongue though, long enough for the single stubs to stop appearing. He stopped going and that was all she needed to know. But she kept the tickets. There were seven. They marked the number of visits her Sid made to Reeny Mosley. Alice sees all this in the turn of the tiny storm and her hand reaches into her pocket.

David pushes his fringe from his face. 'It's beautiful,' he says. It is Liz's face that forms, for just a fraction, in the clouds and mouths the memory of her words, spoken just the night before, words that sent David wandering the streets of High Town long after the last bus carried her home, words that left him sleeping on a bench. As the cloud-face mutely shapes the words, David speaks them aloud. 'I don't want to see you anymore,' he says and like that the face is gone as quick as it takes to tell – quicker – and the storm turns and David smiles once more at the tiny beauty of it. Already beginning to forget Liz Layton, his thoughts turn to other girls.

At the same time, Emily speaks. 'A miracle,' she says, the words muffled by the hand covering her mouth. To her the roil of the cloud is the energy and flare of feelings she has kept too long locked up within her chest, her form forced to quake with unexpressed longing. Emily Blakemore, librarian and spinster, has watched Cyril Renshaw from afar for many years, her feelings for him buttoned tight inside her like a child's treasure in a secret pocket. If one were to check her borrowing history against that of Mr Renshaw it would show she is long in the habit of borrowing each of his selections upon their return to the library. Each book Cyril borrows he deco-rates with marginalia, his thoughts scribbled with HB pencil in the white space of each page. Emily, taking the books home, pours over his comments, rubbing them from page after page to save him the fine. She writes the best of his thoughts down in her diary, replies to them in ink on bound paper, scripting imagined conversations in the soft light of her reading lamp, knowing that speaking to him would really be the most impossible thing in the world. It takes the turn of the storm to move her eyes to Cyril's. He too has seen her love for him in the motion of it and he returns her gaze. Her knees buckle. She gasps and staggers to a chair, Clarence leaping to her lap as she lands on the seat.

'Are you all right Miss?' Cyril asks, stepping to her with eager concern.

'I . . . it . . . I . . . yes,' Emily squeaks, her eyes wide and darting as a hare's.

With all eyes on Emily no one notices the colour drain from Sid's face or hears him whisper to himself, 'Bloody fool,' as he stares into the dark insides of the clouds. There he sees just how much he loves his wife and each thunderclap is a reprimand. He is surprised to find he has forgotten the name of the woman. He didn't expect that, to forget someone who had once seemed so important. He thinks how lucky he is Alice never found out just where it was he slipped out to those Saturday afternoons in the summer of '51. He never thinks of those moments but he is thinking of them now, watching the storm. Inside Sid a low pressure of gratitude meets a high pressure of relief and his heart thunders at the sordid stupidity of his younger self.

'That thing ain't right,' Sid bellows. He marches into

the kitchen returning with the heavy fireplace tongs, waving them in front of him like a toy sword.

'Sidney Stout, what in giddy goodness do you think you're doing?' Alice says, stepping into his path. 'You leave it be for a minute.'

'Quite right,' Cyril says and places himself alongside Alice, between the cup and Sid.

'That thing ain't natural,' Sid shouts, trying to sidestep the pair.

'I must insist you stop.' Cyril moves to once more block Sid's approach.

'This is my café, so it's my say so.' Sid waves the tongs in Cyril's face. 'Get out me way or I'll wrap these round your noggin.'

'Sidney Stout.'

Cyril takes a step to Sid. Their heated breath mingles in the air where their cold stares meet.

'You desperate for a beltin?' Sid waggles the tongs at Cyril once more, his head pecking back and forth like a furious pigeon, but Alice steps in and yanks them from his hand.

'You daft apath, give me those.'

Sid squeals as Alice takes his ear in her fist and pulls him toward the kitchen.

'Your café is it? Do as you please will you, Sidney Stout?'

'Alice, let me loose right now,' he blusters, which only makes her twist all the harder.

Cyril turns to find Emily stood beside him, gazing at him as if he's just fought off a lion.

'Don't let him fluster you, Mr Renshaw,' she says, her

face puffed with admiration. 'Violence is the desperate act of the fearful, the cowardly, the uncivilised.'

Cyril recognises the words as his own scribbled, marginalised thoughts. His head is a flurry of confused realisation and Emily, in a moment of unforeseen bravery, takes his hand in hers.

'Miss Blakemore?'

Cyril watches her smile. He has not seen her do this in all his visits to the library, their brief blurted conversations punctuated instead by the thump of the date stamp.

'Mr Renshaw.'

And the flush of feeling bursts about them both, pulsing with the rising shouts of Sid and Alice in the kitchen and the call and reply of the lightning and thunder bouncing out of the cup.

None of the others notice Tommy pull up a chair and seat himself next to the counter, his eyes level with the cup. The furious churn of the storm grips him. He hears a hurried tinkling as tiny fists of hail sugar the bottom of the cup. For the first time in years he does not think of Alice. The storm's rumble elongates, thunder and lightening overlapping. A tinny crescendo rattles inside the ceramic shelter of the cup. Tommy looks about the café as he rolls himself a fag. The suit and the wallflower lean into each other gripped in some picture house fantasy of love. The young lad sits back at his table drinking the last of his coffee, a stupid grin upon his face. The shouting from the kitchen rolls along, fueled by years of the same air rolling about the system, throwing up the same arguments and the same passions, the same lows and highs.

Tommy thinks of the low pressure deep inside him, heated by years of watching Alice with Sid. Feeling the storm inside him building, his eyes rest back upon the teacup and he tucks the finished roll-up behind his ear for later. Lightning illuminates his face like a lightbulb filament overpowered by a surge of electricity: a flash and then blackness. Tommy doesn't think at this point. He simply raises the cup to his lips and drinks down the storm, rain and hail and all. Cloud moustaches his top lip. A ragged fork of lightning numbs his tongue, filling his mouth with the taste of metal.

A silence falls over the café and all heads turn to him as Tommy drains the last of the storm from the teacup. He licks his lips, wipes them with the back of his hand to remove the last of the cloud.

'What did it taste like?'

It is Alice who asks. Tommy stands mute for a moment then burps, an invisible cloud of ionized air spreading from him, charged like the sky after a storm.

'Like falling in and out of love,' he says.

They sit around a table, all eyes on the once more empty and unremarkable teacup placed in the middle. The atmosphere, the hush, the shared quiet, is fresh and speaks of change and clear skies and new beginnings.

Cyril and Emily hold hands beneath the table, fingers

wrapping and unwrapping each other as if checking and rechecking they are still there.

Alice thumbs the ticket stubs in the pocket of her apron, rolls each one into a tight ball.

David runs his fingers through his hair, pushes his fringe from his eyes, still smiling.

Sid breathes deeply and, pulling Alice's hand from her pocket, he holds it tight.

The storm winds through the complicated path of Tommy's digestive system, the cold simplicity of it over-whelming the frazzling heat of his unrequited love. He picks up the cup from the table, slips it into the pocket of his tattered jacket and, taking the roll-up from behind his ear and lighting it, he leaves without a word. He will not think of Alice at all when, later, he remembers back to the day he swallowed a storm.

Sid strokes the back of Alice's hand with his thumb and she turns to him.

David's eyes close, and his head folds into his arms on the table. He dozes in the sun that beats through the yellowed net across the café window.

Alice whispers 'Still love me?' in Sid's ear. She knows his reply before he gives it.

Cyril and Emily, still holding hands, slip out into the day going on outside. He will walk her to the library this morning, though it is not on his way to work. This evening he will select six books and wait for the library to close, then walk her home.

Sid moves back to the kitchen but not before pulling Alice to him. Their kiss feels, to both of them, like the old days. For just a moment their lips, if not the rest of them, are young again and innocent.

Alice waits until Sid is back at the sink before she begins to clear the tables. She scrapes leftovers from butter-smeared plates. Looking up, to be sure Sid is not watching, she takes the balled-up ticket stubs from her pocket and, one by one, drops them into the bin.

ALLIE ROGERS

COOL FOR CATS

SASHA FOUND THE place where the fence curled away from the metal post and she dared the others. There, in the park keeper's territory, they swore secrecy, passed a bottle of Panda Pop – cherry flavour – and went home on bouncing feet.

Putting on her Wombles pyjamas she could hear her brother's radio. 'At number two in the chart . . . ' Sasha climbed on the bed and hopped from foot to foot, singing along to snatches of words,

'and Davy Crockett rides around and says it's cool for cats, it's cool for cats'.

So that was the name. They passed notes before the bell. 'Going down COOL FOR CATS.' Sasha wrote it up her arm in felt-tip and got sent to the toilets to wash it off.

June wasn't in on Cool for Cats. June was weird. She had American parents and big teeth. If you went to her party you had to say grace. But Sasha liked her lispy voice and the way her dresses hung off her shoulders. She wanted to touch her big hands and her thin, blonde hair.

Sasha was lying under the slide waiting for someone.

The sun was making the pavement wobble. June shimmered.

'You coming to play?'

Sasha reckoned if she'd found it then she could share it if she wanted. The shade was deep in Cool for Cats. June sat all hunched against the cobwebby bushes – stretching her flowery dress across her back. Sasha looked down at the scrappy grass and June's bare thigh. Little lines crisscrossed the skin. Pale pink on the white and redder ones above.

'What's that?'

June tugged her dress down.

'Just where I got a whippin'.'

Sasha looked up at the patch of bright blue sky and away at the corner with the greasy mower and sharp shears. Everything was swimming. A kid was screaming. Something was beating up Sasha's throat like an animal. She shoved her sweaty fingers into the pocket of her shorts, digging.

'D'you want a Frutella? They're blackcurrant.'

June held out her palm and in it Sasha placed the whole, battered packet.

CHERISE SAYWELL

HARD SHOULDER

I ARRIVE NEAR dusk. I've hitched from Glasgow and
walked the last mile. There's grit in my boots and my
trouser hems are filthy but nothing that'd draw your eye.

This is a northern style resort, with tartan in the lobbies
and conifers round the car park. There's a gift shop with
wide glass windows, and a billboard with a film poster on
it. A giant widescreen monitor is mounted outside, dis-
playing images of all the services this resort has to offer
– Spa Suite, Leisure Arena, onsite restaurant – all the separate buildings and what they're called. But I don't need
a map. I know this place.

People are unpacking and checking in at the reception. Skiers. Snowboarders. Families. You can see them
lifting their gear off the racks of SUVs, lining up in the
lobby patting their credit cards against their waterproofs.
It's the weekend. March. They're here for the last of the
snow. Soon it'll be gone.

The ones with money stay in the lodges, lighting their
woodstoves and ordering in food. There's a woman who

comes to cook for them. If I pass her on the road she looks like she knows me but she never says anything.

The ones with less to spend get a room in one of the hotel blocks: Erskine for upmarket, Macarthur for budget and conferences.

My best chance for a meal is the Macarthur block. But not in this state. Not with the dirty trousers, the grubby fingernails. I want to blend in.

The girl on the reception at the Leisure Arena is sitting on a bar stool behind the glass counter. Her mouth is tiny, like all her face is falling into it. She's on the phone, sounding maybe Polish or Ukrainian. They're often from there now. Not like when I used to come.

I take the pen. 'I'm just using the pool,' I murmur. I write first a name, bunching my fingers around the pen. Then a room. 'E', I write, for 'Erskine'. '337'. I scrawl it so the numbers can be mistaken if scrutinised.

Without looking the girl passes me a towel. Then she goes back to her caller.

In the change rooms, the warmth is tropical. You can't believe it's cold outside. People mill about, slopping in from the pool, dripping chlorinated water. Children shout.

I keep my things in a zip-sealed bag: a clean pair of trousers, knickers and a crease-free blouse, a chamois and a pair of plimsolls. My swimsuit's too big but it's only for the walk between the change room and the shower cubicles.

The water comes on hot like always.

I strip, pump the lemon-scented soap in the dispenser

fixed to the wall. There's shampoo, too. The fittings are rusted, probably by chlorine, and the grout is a dirty shade of grey. It'd feel a bit seaside if the tiles weren't so clean. I shampoo my hair, using the pads of my fingers to massage my scalp. I scrape the dirt from under my nails.

When I'm done I wash my travel clothes, soaping the filthy hem of the trousers and scrubbing under the arms of the shirt. Then I dress and put my clothes through the costume wringer. I hang them in a locker using the token I keep safe for this purpose. The key, on its bright elastic band, goes around my arm, pushed up high where nobody will see.

Sometimes when I have to stop, I go to the motorway services. There's one off Junction 7 that has a shower block. I use my chamois to dry myself then. And afterwards, if I have money, I'll buy a coffee. But there's nowhere to clean my clothes, and nowhere to lie down. Mostly I just keep going, sleeping when I can: in cars, homeless hostels if they're not too far from the bypass, very occasionally somewhere like this. It's only a mile off the motorway. I have to be close to the road, but feeling warm and clean and dry like this makes me wish I could stop, swim in the pool, and sleep in a hotel bed with crisp white sheets. But there are rules now and I must keep to them.

When I've found a place to sleep I'll come back and get my clothes. I'll put them on a radiator so they don't dry dank.

Macarthur is warm and quiet. In January when it's heaving they use the ground floor as a lobby, with a satellite check-in so guests won't have to cross the car park from the main building. Now there's just a vending machine and a stand with tourist information beside the counter.

Further along is a door. I turn the handle and when it lets me in I find a function suite with an empty bar in the middle. There are armchairs and couches behind it, tables stacked under dust-sheets. I pull one of them over a dark green sofa. It makes a perfect sleeping place.

High up is a window and on my toes I can see past the car park to the reception building with the television monitor. The advertisements have stopped and there's a news programme with a factory burning on the edge of a field. Beyond the field is a river. A hole has blown out the side of the building and a thick dark substance leaks across a concrete forecourt. A helicopter circles over. Then there's an aerial view of the motorway near the factory, blocked off with miles of cars jammed up. Finally there's a close-up of some workers being winched away.

I wonder how long that road will be closed. I imagine myself behind a wheel, accelerating. I always loved the motorway. Sliproads and bypasses and junctions by number. The arterial pull and how you can be carried high up and still somehow connected to everything you might want. Malls and hotels. Carparks and service stops. You never have to be lost.

I return to my sofa. The radiator's on. I'll get my things from the Leisure locker in the morning.

I tuck my bag behind my sleeping place for safekeeping.

Next I'll find my meal ticket.

∾

Upstairs in Macarthur the doors line up in rows. There are pictures of castles between each one, framed in black acrylic. The walls are papered in a warm ivory tone. The carpet is red and wants to pull me down to it but I keep going.

On the first floor a woman with two small boys carries Tesco bags full of crisps and cartons of juice. You can tell they're destined for the family restaurant. They'll be here on the Special Deal – dinner-bed-and-breakfast, all in. They'll be getting their money's worth. I pass by and head for the next floor where I see a man lugging skis and poles along the corridor. I don't slow down. His jeans bag at the knees; his fleece looks cheap. Everything about him shouts budget.

I know the sort of person I'm looking for. It can take a while but I always spot them a mile off. This time it's a couple on the fourth floor. She's thin and wears expensive-looking boots. Her hair is straight, threaded with subtle highlights. The man is kitted out in ski-wear. They belong in the lodges. At worst, in a luxury Erskine room. They'll have booked late and missed out on the better accommodation. They'll be here on a special deal they don't want.

'We could drive to Ettersley House,' she's saying. 'It's only nine miles.' Her vowels are crisp and round.

'I won't be able to drink.'

'Come on,' she says.

He sighs. You can tell he's used to giving in to her.

She slides a room-card down the swipe lock.

'You can have one with dinner,' she says. 'We'll bring a bottle back and drink it in bed.'

I slow down, as if I'm looking for my card.

They're going into Room 458.

'Alright,' he agrees.

The door closes. She laughs behind it.

Room 458, I note.

Then I go back downstairs.

I'm doing all the right things. To move invisibly around a place like this you only have to know where to put your feet: the right places to pause and where you must not stop. If you look lost, someone will ask and then you'll come into focus. You'll have to explain.

It's like being on the motorway. Who will remember your car unless it stops? Who will remember the way the wheels turned, the pattern on the hubcaps or how the paint was scratched at the back. No one will notice unless your car cuts in front of another, or weaves drunkenly towards the barrier, or stops on the hard shoulder. Remember what you have learned, I tell myself. Keep moving, and if you need to stop, do it gradually, signalling your intention. Then no one will notice you're dirty. They won't remember what you've done, or where you've come from. They won't wonder where you're sleeping.

You can never go back.

The first thing to go wrong is the snow. I don't see it until I'm back downstairs. It's late in the season for such a thick new covering. It hardly ever falls this far down the mountain after February. But now it lies everywhere in a soft-solid layer, too cold for plimsolls, hiding all the things I need to see to keep my bearings. I'm not ready for it, and I know I should go and get my things from the locker and find the gritted road, black and stark. It will be waiting for me.

But I don't. I want to rest a while. I'm so hungry. So tired. I stay in my secret place behind the bar and listen out for the 458ers passing through the foyer on their way to the Ettersley. Occasionally I stand on my toes and look out the window at the car park. I try and guess which one is theirs – something small and sporty with a roof rack for their skis. They'll move expertly through the snow. It won't bother them at all. She'll be all easy glamour – maybe a wraparound dress in silk jersey beneath a well-lined coat. Knee-high boots with a neat block heel. Nothing silly. She's got the sort of body that likes in and out of clothes easily.

Families chatter by, crossing the silent car park to the restaurant. A group of teenagers. A few couples, but not the 458ers. I watch until it's nearly eight o'clock and then I think they must have left another way.

I consider the cold, my thin plimsolls, and I decide to head to the restaurant now, while the snow's fresh and can be brushed away easily. I'm so hungry I'm faint.

But when I emerge from my secret place another bad thing happens.

A man comes out of the stairway just as I'm closing the bar room door. He's in staff uniform, and maybe it's the shock but I do the worst possible thing. I stop. I just stand there with my legs soft as porridge. His eyes travel over me; then he looks past me, at the closed-up bar. I turn and shut the door. Without speaking, he continues on his way and I allow myself to believe he thought nothing at all of me coming out of that empty suite: a guest taking the wrong door, entering a room in error.

To calm myself I detour into the stairwell. I go up two flights and along a corridor. *You're going to dinner*, I tell myself. *You were on your way when you opened the wrong door.* I put one foot in front of the other. *You're going to eat in the family restaurant. It's included in your Special Deal.*

I turn and go back downstairs.

'Room 458,' I announce at the front desk in the family restaurant. 'Macarthur.' The sound of my voice surprises me, not loud, but it knows its business.

The girl behind the desk has an accent just like the girl in Leisure.

'Special Deal?' she asks.

'That's right.'

'Then your dinner is included.' She speaks with precision. She enunciates every word.

'Yes,' I say.

'But you will have to pay for alcoholic drinks.'

'Can I settle any extras with a credit card?' I ask, for good measure.

'Of course,' she says. 'Hilde will show you to your table.'

The Special Deal includes two courses plus coffee and Hilde's quick taking my order. I choose the Tagliatelle with Carbonara, wanting starch and fat to fill me, to line my stomach and fortify. The cream has split, and tiny drops of oil pool in the sauce. The bacon is slivered and the pasta is so soft that it breaks around my fork. I use a spoon, going slowly.

Across the room Hilde serves a pair of young snow-boarders with bowls of ravioli. When I'm done, I don't put my hand up to get her attention. I push my empty plate away and wait.

'Was everything okay?'

The voice belongs to a man, not Hilde.

I note the badge first. The name: Stan. Then the face, blank, neutral, as though he never saw me nearly an hour ago in the doorway outside the function suite. He takes my plate.

'Yes,' I say. 'It was lovely.'

'Would you like a dessert?'

'I'd like the panna cotta and a coffee please.'

He moves in closer, murmurs, 'Would you like them together? Because if you like, you can have coffee in your room.' His breath tickles my skin and I shiver. There's too much food in my stomach. Panic sours the pleasure of it.

I make my voice calm and answer without hesitating. 'You made a mistake,' I say. I look right at him. 'There's no room service with the Special Deal. I'd like my coffee and panna cotta here, please.'

'Of course,' he says.

It's hard to finish the dessert with the claw of worry in my stomach, and after I'm done an old instinct returns, to wash it down with something that will soften the edges and speed up the night. But I don't, and it's a good thing too, because I need my wits about me almost right away.

I go along to the desk, already thinking ahead to collecting my things from the Leisure locker, my bag from

Macarthur. I'll brush my teeth, but that's all. Then there'll
be the road, waiting for me.

'Room 458,' I announce to the girl on the desk. I have
the bill in my hand, so she can mark it down and confirm
that the meal is covered.

But she pauses and puts her finger on the bookings
page, checks the screen on her computer, and I begin to
tremble because in the corner of my eye the 458ers are
striding towards a table. They have not gone to Ettersley
House. Perhaps it's the snow. They have stayed and sub-
mitted to the budget menu.

'Oh,' the girl on the desk says to me, 'it can't be 458. Can
I have your room key? I'll scan it and check the number.'

'It's alright,' I murmur. 'I've got it here somewhere . . .'
I move out of the way, eyeing the door as if it might save
me.

But then Stan is there beside me. 'Her room is 495,'
he says, his accent rolled up and delivered from somewhere in the back in his throat. He looks at me and shrugs
lightly. 'It is an easy mistake to make.'

'Yes,' I say. 'An easy mistake.' I step backwards. 'Sorry
about that.'

I hurry to the Leisure Arena. I have that hurting feeling
from moving too fast with a stomach full of food. My jaw
aches like marbles are shoved under my tongue. I fall in
the snow and bruise my hip. I didn't pay attention and
now everything is wrong. I have to leave this place.

But then, worst of all, the Leisure Arena is closed.
Through the huge glass window the water lies perfectly

still. The night-lights are on and there's nobody about to open the door.

I notice dimly that my feet are cold inside the plimsolls. Snow is caked up the sides of them. Without proper shoes, I won't get far.

Defeated, I make my way across the car park to Macarthur. The widescreen television at the reception is still on, even though there's no one about. Distantly I hear it. News again, with that burning factory and the chemical spill, clouds of black clotting the air. Something dark leaches into the earth. There's an aerial view, with the field and river on the other side of the factory, buildings and then houses before the motorway, then a cutaway to two men arguing about who is to blame. Who will pay for all this mess? A young man with a beard comes on. He holds a cloth over his mouth. He points to the field. The river. He says the damage is worse than can be seen.

I turn and hurry across the car park, scuttling into Macarthur, to my hidey-hole bed, knowing I won't sleep a wink tonight.

It's nearly midnight when Stan comes. I've lain fully dressed under the dustsheet, knowing that he will. The door whispers on its hinges and I hold perfectly still, waiting to see what he'll do. Maybe hand me over to someone – I might finish the night in a cell. That's not so bad. It's nothing new. But it's more likely Stan will want something for himself first.

'Come,' he says, without moving any closer. 'Come with me.'

'I need my things,' I say, rising. 'My shoes. Please? I left them in Leisure. In a locker.'

'You can have your things,' he says. 'Later.' His voice slips quietly into the dark space between us. 'First, we go upstairs.'

I carry my damp plimsolls and walk in my socks, passing doors distinguishable only by numbers. The 458ers are silent behind theirs. I lower my head, keeping my eyes level. At the end of the corridor we pass into another wing: more doors until the last one. It has no number. Stan takes a card from his belt and draws it deliberately down the reader. Inside is a room with a bed and a chair, a television, a basin, a shower.

'Later,' he says, 'you may sleep in the bed. Use the shower. I have laid clean sheets.'

I wait to see what he'll do.

'Put your bag down,' he says.

'Is this your room?' I ask.

'No,' he says. 'I have my own room. In the Staff Lodge.' He thumbs in the direction of the window. 'Over there.'

'Why don't we go there?'

'This is more private.'

I grip my bag.

'We will get your things from the Leisure Arena now,' Stan says. 'But you should leave your bag here'.

It's only got a few things in it: spare socks, a purse with five or six coins, a cardigan. Not much, but not easy for me to replace.

He knows I won't go without it. He'll have what he wants.

I close my eyes and think of the hard shoulder. I picture

a woman standing there. I remind myself it's only what I owe. I mustn't forget.

I put my bag down.

'Come on,' he says.

We cross the car park in silence, snow catching in our hair. The sky is rubbed orange by the fingers of light reaching up from the resort.

I stare into all the empty cars as I pass them. The people who come to this place always drive. They can't get here any other way with all the stuff they carry. Tyres squeezed beneath helmets and skis and boots and poles and gloves. Luggage on racks: gear in the back. You see them heading up the motorway. Sometimes they have so much they can't see out their rear windows. It doesn't matter, they'll be thinking. It's only one journey. Fifty, sixty, a hundred kilometres: the smoothness of the one-way, the ribbon of road.

When we get to Leisure, Stan punches in a code and pushes the door. He points me in the direction of the change rooms and follows, his footfall soft and heavy.

I take my things from the locker and replace the key. I feel better once I can hold it all. I feel ready for whatever's coming. 'I suppose you'll be wanting it back in that room,' I say, turning.

He grips my arm. 'No,' he says. 'We will go in here.' He ushers me in to where the pool is. The light is low and deep; water slurps softly against the tiles. The snow has stopped now and outside the whole world is thick and pale and hidden.

Stan strips to his underwear and I look away and wait for his instruction.

He slips into the water.

'It's nice,' he says. 'It's good to be here when there's no one.' His words vibrate in the hollow silence.

'Yes,' I say, dryly, because I'm not doing anything in the pool. I'm wondering if he's sorted out that room so he can make good use of me.

He begins to swim, doing first a clumsy front crawl, then a slow breast-stroke. After he's swum a half a dozen laps, he stops.

'You can come in if you wish,' he says. 'No one will see.'

'I'd rather not,' I say. But to placate him I walk to the edge and remove my shoes, roll my trousers to my knees and lower my feet, swilling the water around them.

'Are you without a home,' he asks, coming closer.

'Kind of.'

'A traveller?'

I shrug. 'Sometimes.' The water makes patterns out of the low light on the ceiling. 'Are you allowed in here?' I ask.

'Like you,' he says. 'No one has said I can't. I am a staff supervisor. I have all the keys. It is easy enough if I am discreet.'

'I thought you worked in the restaurant.'

'I have more than one position. I make myself . . .' he pauses, searching for the word, '. . . versatile.'

The water is blood-warm, outlining my skin only when I move my feet.

'Where do you return to?' he asks. 'When you have finished travelling?'

'Depends,' I say. I deflect his probing. 'Where are you from?'

'Gdansk,' he says.

'Poland?'

'Yes.'

'Is Hilde from Poland?'

'No,' he says. 'Latvia. Some are from Ukraine too.'

'When I used to come here,' I say, 'when I paid to stay, everybody who worked here was from the village.'

Stan shrugs. 'Lucky you didn't need a room then,' he says.

'But the room's not just for me, is it?' I bristle.

'I have my own room,' Stan says. 'I already said that.'

'Why aren't you in Poland?' I ask.

'Here I can work,' he says. 'I make money. I send it home to my wife. My daughter.' He turns on his back, floats. His thin hair spreads out in the water. He's not young, but I can't really tell his age.

'Do you like it here?' I ask when he's upright again.

'No.'

'Can you not work in Gdansk?'

'Maybe,' he says. 'But I'm no good there.' He wades to the ladder, climbs out of the pool and goes to his trousers, retrieving two small bottles, mini-bar sized. He holds them up, vodka and bourbon.

'Will you join me?' he asks. 'The sauna is off now, but there will still be warmth.'

There's nothing in his face I can understand. 'No,' I say, carefully. 'I think I'll wait here.'

He shrugs. 'Okay.' He replaces the bourbon, holds up the vodka. 'I will dry off while I have this. Only one, you see. You will not need to be afraid of me. It is only a small pleasure, you understand?'

'Yes,' I tell him.

Stan props the door of the sauna open with a rolled rubber mat. 'No light,' he says, meeting my eye. 'I don't like the door to be closed with the darkness.'

He pauses and I nod. 'Okay,' I promise. I won't close it on him.

He sits, soaking up the last warmth of the wood, sipping his vodka. It's the way he drinks that makes me rise and go to him: the tiny measured dose and how he rests the top of the bottle against his bottom lip in between each sip. I know how the drink will melt into him, each drop telling him he wants more.

I undress to my underpants and sit beside him. I put my lips on the skin of his shoulder, my hand on his thigh, breathing the anaesthetic scent of the vodka, the woody tang of the sauna.

Gently he removes my hand and holds it in his. 'I watched you in the restaurant,' he says. 'I see how hungry you are. But the way you eat: you take only small mouthfuls. You are accustomed to denying yourself.'

We are silent for a long time. Stan doesn't move to kiss me or cup my breast in his hand. Somewhere inside me is the long-forgotten tremor of wanting and when I sense it's time to go I don't want to part with him. 'Are you going to sleep in the room with me?' I ask.

'No,' he says. 'I mustn't.'

'Okay.'

We dress in silence, our backs to each other. I pull my boots on over dampish socks, thinking of the radiator in the empty room where I'll sleep, and how my clothes will soon be dry after all.

Outside, the snow has stopped. We walk over the thick bed of it. It sighs as our feet compress it.

The reception building is dimly lit. Deep inside, someone swills a mop along a tiled surface. The lights in the display window of the gift shop illuminate the mannequins, poised: dressed already for spring. The widescreen monitor is switched off.

'Tomorrow,' Stan says, 'it will be seven degrees. This snow will be gone by afternoon. Where will you be then?'

'On the motorway,' I tell him. I breathe the sharp cold air.

'Where are you going?' he asks.

'I'm not sure.'

'How did you get here?'

'I got dropped off nearby, and then I walked.'

He nods and waits and I want to tell him about the places where I ask to get out. Where ever flowers have been left. Often they're still wrapped in cellophane, tied to the metal barrier, or to a street lamp or a pole.

'Sometimes I stop,' I say. 'I have to. It's like, a rule.'

I remember each place, even after the flowers are gone. The first is less than a mile from here.

'Did you see the news today?' I ask.

'No,' he says.

'There was a fire. In a factory. A lot of damage. I thought I might go there.'

Stan frowns. He wants to understand.

'You should have your own car,' he says, 'to be moving about, always, like that.'

'I used to,' I say. I think about the beginning of this journey. How it was only a moment. Blood hot with vodka. Head full of all the things I wanted. It was never enough. I want to explain, to repay him for his kindness. But I can't.

We walk in silence until we reach the room. Stan swishes the keycard down the slot. 'It's best if you leave in the morning,' he says. 'You can return, but I can't do this again.'

'Okay.'

He presses the keycard into my hand. 'Put this under the door when you leave.'

He touches my face. Then he goes.

I lay my things over the radiator. I use the toilet and brush my teeth in the sink. I put the bar of soap in my bag, the shampoo and toothpaste. Only the things I need.

I lie down in the bed. Maybe I sleep. Perhaps it is a dream. There's snow outside but I'm warm in my car; there's grit on the road, the tyres grip the tarmac. I've had a drink and everything is sharp and clear. There are bends but they're smooth and easy. I can go a little wide, there's still the hard shoulder. I'm doing nearly eighty. It doesn't feel fast.

A woman waves. She's standing near the barrier. What is she doing there? If I could reach her I could tell her. But I can't stop. Not now. Everything is moving so fast. Soon there'll be an exit, or a sign, something to tell me where I should go next.

AIDAN SEMMENS

ARK OF MARVELS

A portrait of Julius Caesar, a looking-glass,
an African charm entirely made of teeth,
a north American canoe & a stone axe,
Napoleon's silver-handled toothbrush, a sign
from a Viennese apothecary's shop,
the bell & bauble of King Henry's fool,
a Dutch still-life, a bust of Attila the Hun,
a Madonna fashioned in feathers from Indian birds,
a needlework map of Britain, a striking likeness
of Moses, an organ in mother-of-pearl, a clock
with a mighty Ethiop riding astride a rhino,
a sundial shaped like a monkey, a mermaid's hand,
the tail, but not the horn, of a unicorn,
a pair of Galapagos terns & a taxidermed booby,
the last known dodo, an array of shoes
in every global style, a cunning machine
for translating sounds to colours,
a Chinese torture chair of lethal blades,
a fine-carved Aztec sacrificial knife,

prosthetic limbs in polished wood & leather,
a pile of amputation saws, a device
for preventing masturbation (nickel-plated),
a brass corset, a chastity-belt of iron,
the mummified corpse of a young Peruvian boy,
an ivory model of a pregnant woman (open),
a case of assorted implements for birth,
a glass syringe, a guillotine blade (used),
a snuffbox in the head of a horned ram,
a dentist's signboard strung with 100 teeth,
the moccasins worn by Florence Nightingale,
three tons of worthless metal, five of old photos,
two of wood boulders, Darwin's walking-stick,
a case of 50 glass eyes, a wooden leg,
many useless tools, some obsolete hoists,
three and a half tons of swords, two and a half of guns,
cannons, helmets & shields, 110 cases
of Greco-Roman artefacts, 85
of surgical instruments, 60 of pestles & mortars,
a hoard of gourds from Guatemala &
an urn containing the ashes of the collector.

JOSE VARGHESE

ARGUMENTATIVE HANDS

IT WAS A drizzle that confused everyone. The musicians and artists didn't know whether to pack up and go home, or to wait till it went away. The bridge seemed empty all of a sudden, with people rushing past each other to find a place where they could escape the unexpected rain-drops. We were in the middle of all that, too busy to notice anything. We were having an argument, if you remember. That was how things used to work for us. How I wish we retained that reckless spirit of our youth. Now, we get tired of arguments faster than they reach anywhere.

The spot where you kissed on my cheek still felt warm. It was soon after the kiss that we allowed ourselves to be lost in the meaningless argument. I don't remember what it was about, but the image of the bridge and our agitated selves stuck over it in the rain still remains fresh in my mind.

We were meant to be stuck in places, through the seasons. We thought of each other as mere impossibilities in our life, but we got stuck somewhere. Was it the passion that we had for finding fault with each other? Or was it just the realization that there couldn't be a better one waiting for us in the near or distant future? We were too ordinary, with no exceptionally striking facial features or great bodies. But that was what drew us together, perhaps.

Now my aged hands tremble more than yours. You try to hold them in vain. You may survive this winter, but I am not sure about me. The chill that escapes into our modest apartment through the gaps in our windows makes me shiver. Sometimes the shivering scares you, but you look at my eyes intently and try to hold my hands. Our hands tremble, like two young people in the heat of an argument. You look surprised as I smile. And then you smile, as if you have searched out the image of us in the hands, from my blurry thoughts.

JUDI WALSH

VICTOR

THEY CRACK THE quiet sheen of politeness in the carriage. The other passengers have been sitting, or hanging from a pole rooted to the ground, staring at their own thoughts, minding their own business. The doors open and the three of them step in. They take up space, take up ownership. Now they have arrived, the others look elsewhere: past them, at each other, out of the window to the black wall beyond. With wooden smiles, the passengers sit smaller in their seats, drawing their possessions close, careful not to draw attention to themselves. They are uncomfortable, and he likes that.

They laugh hard and swear. The other passengers don't use that language; he watches them wince with every fuck. He slaps his hand on the window to see them jump. He knows that they are scared. He turns to his girl with an arrogant swagger, but she shifts all her weight to face the other lad, lifting her head, exposing her neck, and his smile flickers. The other lad gestures to him with a bottle, like a sabre, pointing and waving it in commanding invitation. He bites down hard to remove the top, like so many times before. It is his thing. No big deal. He returns the bottle, shrugging his shoulders. His girl and the other lad share a look that he doesn't see.

They sit and he stands, and they all laugh and swear together. He sucks his lip over and over, but doesn't raise his hand to wipe. The metallic taste of his blood is still there when the doors open for their stop.

ADAM WILSHAW

FLOWERS, WHISKY

MY SON BROUGHT me flowers when he was a child. He cut them with his fingers from the garden by the greenhouse. Weeds, roses, dandelions. These are for you, he said. Now he's much older than I was then and he's brought me flowers again.

I can see the garden here through the window in the dining room. It has concrete beds and grass painted with mud and bird shit. It's too small for me and I have to stay indoors.

I stay in here and my son holds my hand in a different way. When he was the child I held his hand when we walked, to stop him running in the road or falling off a wall. Now he holds my hand to stop me going away.

He puts the flowers in a vase on the table next to my bed. In the summer when he was four-years-old he picked the weeds and brought them to me and said, these are for you, mummy. I put them in a vase on the table next to my bed. That was when we were in a timeless state, the slack water, before time really started to move. Happiness is a timeless state. When he brought me the flowers he looked shy and proud. I lifted him and kissed him. He smelled of the warm of his bed, like rising bread dough and sweat and urine. These things are not abstractions when they are your child. They are love itself.

Now the only time I feel detached from death is during the hour before he arrives, when I know that sadness is time. That's when I can fool myself with something I guess is hope, if hope is an animal running circles in your belly.

That's when I remember the smooth of his skin and his hair wet from the bath. In his towel in my arms he would put his head to my breast through my clothes and his feet would be clean and cold. I would put him on the bed and talc his body and that was the only time he ever showed doubt, the only time I could see revealed any awareness of the vulnerability of being someone's child. I would think how easy it would be to pass on pain in its DNA. I would run through horrors and that was my unconscious protecting me from the future. If he had been electrocuted by my hairdryer, or killed in a storm, or routed by cancer, or a bus, or a bomb, then something in me would want me to continue, even when oblivion would be the only option after something so easily imaginable.

It's normal to worry about your baby, I was told. But you must keep some thoughts away, I was told, because your thoughts are sometimes too dark. I thought of that advice when I sat in the dark of my room with the window which looked to the sea, when the sea was invisible.

Like me now, fixed to a soft chair, like a parasite which

gains strength from its own weakness, he covered his fear with innocent smiles, because we were attached. All those baby things, when your body leaves your body and becomes thought, become part of your death. The blood, the vomit, the animal attachments. We begin with lust and end with defeat. Doctors give me sweets and tickle my toes but they can't inoculate me from the sickness of days and age. But I didn't know it when I was young because I didn't know I was young when I was young, and now he is like me, now.

Before I woke this morning I was a girl collecting flowers from my mother's garden before my father came home. It was a cold morning and the dandelions had no smell. I snipped the stems with my fingernails and held them in a green squeak of palm. I was wearing my night-dress and slippers. She was in the kitchen, reading. I left the flowers on the table and she said, thank you Maria, without looking at me. When she bathed me it was quick. Toys were not allowed. Singing, shouting, boys, and questions gave her an ache. I was washed and dried without fuss, like a good child. She had spent so much time waiting for my father that her personality had become warped into a shell of permanent frustrated impatience. The only time she would play with me was when I was completing a jigsaw puzzle and now I know why. I was sure she loved me but regretted me, which I think is fair.

The doctor told me it wasn't fair. I had a right to be loved, he said with a straight face, and there was no need for my life to be such a painful calculation. I looked at him and imagined him naked. He was twice my age and I thought of his legs as the wrinkled branches of a tree and his belly as a furry coconut and his manhood as a baby's acorn. He said my laughter showed I had failed to engage with my problem. Do you think your child would be happy if you went away again, he asked me. I didn't stop laughing. I wanted to tell him that I didn't know before that moment that you are attached to death the moment your father's sperm finds the right egg in your mother's womb and you stay attached forever. I know it's all a mirage, this love, this hope. Your child will move, run. You teach, you think, your child. You think too much of yourself. There's sun, then cloud. He's a man but I can see the boy.

He doesn't know what to say. You don't teach your child to talk to its dying mother. You teach them nothing, really, because they teach themselves. We tell ourselves such grand lies about our children. We take credit where it is not due. I cannot run, or swim, or cycle, or throw a ball. When he was a boy he could run so fast I struggled to catch him. He was in the teams, my sister told me: hockey; football; athletics. When he fell asleep I would wait, just in case, as if I might be able to save him. And when he grew too much for me to carry him, I folded like a bleak joke.

I refused to continue his childish routines and games, even though he loved them, because I thought he should grow up. They change so quickly; that's what people say about children. But it's not true of your own children.

Your own children never change. From the moment you create and then witness their first indignity, birth, and throughout all the love and compromises of their life, they remain precisely the same. They do not change at all and that is why human love is a kind of animal agony. When they fail at school, in friendship, at love, or catch a disease, or break a bone, or commit a crime, or succeed, or have their own children, they remain exactly the same. They do not change. They merely endure another indignity and then another indignity, like their birth, and their birth becomes more of your responsibility with every human second that falls away.

You know, time's weight increases and one day I expect it will become so heavy that the world will spin from its orbit and collide with the moon. My son's experience is too massive for me but it's not as painful as his innocence. Perfection would be to hold my baby in time forever without knowledge of anything.

He brought me flowers from the hedgerow near the beach on the Sunday before he first went to school. The grass there was as sharp as razors. I was distracted and didn't say thank you before I put them in my pocket. He asked me later if I he could put them in a vase but I had thrown them in the bin because their petals were bruised and the stems were weak. He said, it doesn't matter mummy, I can pick some more, you know. He was nervous at school and didn't make friends.

He doesn't know what to say now. I guess we could talk about the things we liked to do, as the nurse suggested. He used to love to dance when he was a child and now he hates to dance. I cannot imagine him trying to dance. He would look like an idiot, with his stocky build and bald head. He is like my father, I think, from what I remember. I might tell him that, to lighten the mood. I hope you're not thinking of dancing! Would he smile? Would he remember? No, a strange thing to say, an indication of dementia. You must keep some thoughts away, I was told, your thoughts are too dark. I thought of that advice when I sat in the dark of my room with the window which looked to the sea, when the sea was invisible.

It's too easy to be sombre in this cabbage place, with its boiled air. It's too tempting to repeat yourself, to curdle memories, to philosophise, to reminisce without purpose. I feel sorry for myself, which I think is fair.

I told him to never feel sorry for himself. You know he once brought me a foxglove and when I warned him it was poisonous he took it outside again. I guessed he had thrown it away but a week later I found he had tried to replant it, lodging its broken limb with pebbles he had collected, and it had already started to rot under the heavy summer rain. It was a December foxglove, an impossible foxglove. Perhaps it was a daisy or a piece of ice from the gutter on the shed. That was the last time he brought me a flower, or anything like that. It was an ending. Giving birth to him was the end of everything for me. No, I'm wrong, he used to hate to dance. I was wrong.

He loved to run. I couldn't catch him, even before he went to school, long before they took him to live with my sister in the city. Then I couldn't catch him in a car or a bus or by the speed of thought. Crying and drinking didn't help me to catch him. He hated dancing, particularly my dancing. My memory is a slippery corridor full of dull bends and bricked doorways. I mean, what I mean, is giving birth to him was the beginning of everything for me and where there is a beginning there is an end because that is the only logic of this world. You know he once brought me an icicle from the gutter of the shed. It was a dagger. The snow had stopped after a fortnight.

That was the last winter we spent in that house. He says he can't remember.

But it's full of light here and the windows are open. I can go through a door into the garden and look in the shed my husband built for us before he had to go, where we kept his pots for the spring. We would plant the seedlings together at the weekend. He was a good boy, a natural boy. He was gentle before he went to the city but he came back different.

He didn't like me drinking so much. I didn't like me drinking so much. But after my husband went, it helped. The experts and the therapists told me it doesn't really help, it just masks the real problem. They're full of shit. It helped. When you go to the dentist you don't refuse the painkiller because it would be wrong to not endure the agony of having a drill rammed into the nerves of your teeth. All the advice I have heard in my life has been a kind of suffocation. All the help has been useless. There are too many people talking at me, even now. They tickle my toes and ask my idiot questions. They tickle my questions in return. That is not human sympathy. We're just like cattle. I wait to see my son but I hope he goes soon, because I'm too tired now to be a mother.

But it was a problem. It started with a drink when he was asleep when he was a small child. Then it was half a bottle. Then it was a bottle. He didn't like the mornings when I couldn't see properly and smelled like dead roses. I didn't like it. I shouted at him. I saw his smile fade.

He brought me flowers as if flowers would always grow there for him to collect and give to me. But maybe that first sadness was there when he saw the dandelions and weeds die a week later. Maybe that was the end of the slack water, when the tides started to move. And if I could I would have stopped everything and held him forever and if I could have done that I would be holding him now with the sun on the sides of the trees and time.

On the beach he always found a shell for me and remembered it a year later, when it was lost.

He's brought me whisky, too, a miniature bottle. I can't drink it but he remembers I drank it. He's searching for ways to be kind and for ways to make himself feel better.

I can't tell him that love is a trick we play on ourselves.

NICHOLAS YH WONG

ZERO COPULA

'To die, to sleep —/ No more . . . 'Tis a consummation/
Devoutly to be wished.'

Hamlet, SHAKESPEARE

Let us just lie down and listen to Richter, you said,
as if measure will save us from any earthquake.
When I became Geryon and unfolded my wings
into the glare of a volcano, your ambition for me
was less mythological. Not Russian prison tattoos,
but a one-inch-long haircut. Like a bat winding in
evolution's cage, I burnt into a cloud, echolocating
the root of my tongue. O let me sleep, and no more
count with obscure knives the cupolas on your chest,
dance with Tanizaki's spider on the hill of your back.
I am Heathcliff, but are you? What seems beloved is.
Yet, you cursed in the garbled white noise of English,
at what linguists call zero copula in our native speak.
A goddess sprung from monkeys' hips, useless since
the category copula is no stain-proof maiden after all.
So do we really need the copula, to be, to be in love?

Jesus wept in other languages too. And so wielding Occam's razor, you pared my sensational Chinese boy head down to its bare treatise. Which copula? The passion according to Johannes de Garlandia.

JAN WOOLF

FIXED

I SHOULD HAVE reprised Ophelia by now, or Nora in A Doll's House, thinks Siobhan, whose last role in a minor soap had been another fall from grace.

'Could you read it again Shervorn,' says Mark, TfL's London North media-manager.

So she does.

'Because of a mechanical fault, the downstairs escalator is out of order. Customers are therefore requested to use the fixed staircase with care.'

'Do you not think you could not snarl like that on *fixed*,' sighs Mark.

'Watch your double negatives darling.'

'Oh for fuck's sake,' he whispers, his eyes finding the ceiling. 'I need to get out of here too. Right?'

'Right.' She looks down at her Jimmy Choos.

'Cue. Take eight,' says Mark, pretending to be a movie director. It helps.

Siobhan gathers herself.

'Because of a mechanical fault the downstairs escalator is out of order. Customers are therefore requested to use the

... 'FIXED?' she shouts, slapping her thigh with the same force she'd slapped it at last year's Wigan panto.

'Just say it Shervorn,' pleads Mark, his eyelids fluttering like moths.

'Of course staircases are bloody fixed,' she snaps. *Someone might recognise my voice at Kentish Town station and I'll want to die* – she doesn't quite say. She looks into his eyes, breathing deeply, 'this is worse than supply teaching.'

'Really?' says Mark, keeping eye contact, trying to recall any of his teachers that had looked as good as her. 'And,' barks Siobhan, 'they're passengers NOT customers.'

'Let's not open a second front,' says Mark with a calm he cannot feel. 'Just say it – and we can both go.'

Where, she thinks, catching a whiff of fresh sweat beneath the aftershave. 'Isn't a bloody cast iron staircase obviously fixed?'

'You're the stare case,' he mutters to himself, finding her eyes very pretty. 'It's health and safety Shervorn.'

'How? Mark.'

He shrugs, shifting his gaze to her breasts. 'The wordage is facilitated by our communications committee.'

'Wordage?'

His tension combusts. 'JUST BLOODY SAY IT.'

'I FANCY THE ARSE OFF YOU.'

'Yes?'

'Yes. Now we can both go . . . .'

'Where?'

JANE YEH

THE FACTS
OF LIFE

Haven't you people heard of lesbians?
What's with this school? Where are the hockey skirts,
The shortie pyjamas, the barely clad girls?
I expect a little more titillation

Before some saccharine lesson is learnt
About friendship or sharing or the value
Of work. I'm not like the others – I'm a new
Kind of girl: part tomboy, part mechanic, part

Up to no good. Give me the airhead with boobs
For a roomie – I'm sure we'll get along.
The blonde and the fat chick can bring up the rear;

I'll show them how we do things in the Bronx.
We've all got the same parts under the hood –
And I'm handy with a spanner. I think I'll like it here.

CONTRIBUTOR
NOTES

CLAIRE ASKEW's poetry has appeared in numerous publications, including *The Guardian, Poetry Scotland, The Edinburgh Review* and *PANK*. She has been twice shortlisted for an Eric Gregory Award (2010, 2012), and in 2012 won a Scottish Book Trust New Writers Award. She is about to graduate from the University of Edinburgh with a PhD in Creative Writing. She teaches creative writing at bookwormtutors.co.uk and blogs at onenightstanzas.com

JENNA BUTLER is the author of three books of poetry, *Seldom Seen Road* (NeWest Press, 2013), *Wells* (University of Alberta Press, 2012), and *Aphelion* (NeWest Press, 2010), in addition to ten short collections with small presses in Canada, the United States, and Europe. Butler teaches at Grant MacEwan University in Alberta, Canada during the school year. In the summer, she and her husband live with three resident moose and a den of coyotes on an organic farm in northern Alberta.

JOANNA CAMPBELL's stories are published in *The New Writer, Writers' Forum, The Yellow Room* and anthologies published by Cinnamon Press, Earlyworks Press, Unbound Press and Biscuit Publishing. Shortlisted three times for the Bridport Prize and twice for Fish, she has a story in the 2010 Bristol Short Story Prize Anthology.

In 2011, she came second in Scottish Writers Association's contest and won the Exeter Writers competition. In 2012 she was shortlisted in Mitchelstown Literary Society's William Trevor/Elizabeth Bowen competition.

ARMANDO CELAYO was born and raised in Oklahoma City, OK, but now lives in Norwich, where he attended the Creative Writing MA at the University of East Anglia. He is at work on a novel titled *For the Recovery of Lost Things*.

SARAH-CLARE CONLON's micro fiction has been published by Comma Press (*The Hat You Wear*), National Flash-Fiction Day (*Jawbreakers*), *Flash: The International Short-Short Story Magazine*, *Ferment Literary Zine*, *The Pygmy Giant* and *Thick Jam*. She performs in spoken word and music act Les Malheureux with author David Gaffney, and organises events and anthologies with writing collective FlashTag. She has written for *Elle* and *Nova* magazines, worked for various cultural organisations, including Manchester Literature Festival, and won awards as a culture blogger.

PHILLIP CRYMBLE lives in Fredericton, New Brunswick, where he serves as a poetry editor for *The Fiddlehead*. A naturalized Canadian born in Belfast, Northern Ireland, he holds a MFA in Creative Writing from the University of Michigan, and will soon begin studying towards a PhD in English. His poems have appeared in *The North*, *Iota*, *Oxford Poetry*, *Poetry Ireland Review*, and numerous other publications worldwide. *Not Even Laughter*, his first full-length collection, will be released by Salmon Poetry in 2014.

PETER DANIELS has twice won the Poetry Business pamphlet competition (1991 and 1999), and came first in the 2002 Ledbury, 2008 Arvon, and 2010 TLS poetry competitions. His first full poetry collection is *Counting Eggs* from Mulfran Press (2012). His translations of Vladislav Khodasevich from Russian are published by Angel Classics (2013). He lives in London and works as a freelance editor.

TIM ERICKSON lives in Salt Lake City, Utah, USA. His poems have appeared in *Chicago Review, Western Humanities Review, Mudfish,* and elsewhere.

KEVLIN HENNEY writes shorts and flashes and drabbles of fiction. His fiction has appeared online and on tree, including with *Litro, New Scientist, Word Gumbo, Fiction365, Dr. Hurley's Snake-oil Cure, Every Day Fiction, The Pygmy Giant* and *Flash Frontier,* and has been included in the *Jawbreakers, Kissing Frankenstein & Other Stories* and *Flash Me!* anthologies. Kevlin also reads his fiction at spoken word events and is the winner of the 2012 Oxford Flash Slam. He lives in Bristol and online.

TANIA HERSHMAN is the author of two story collections: *My Mother Was An Upright Piano: Fictions* (Tangent Books, 2012), a collection of 56 very short fictions, and *The White Road and Other Stories* (Salt, 2008), which was commended, 2009 Orange Award for New Writers). www.taniahershman.com

ANNEMARIE HOEVE spent a frostbitten childhood in

the Canadian prairies followed by a few years of trying to drink milky tea in the UK. She has now settled in Amsterdam, where she works as a freelance writer. Ideas (like the one for the story in this anthology) tend to strike when she is pedalling across town amid the city's 881,000 bikes. Secret fact: she did clog dancing as a child and liked it. For more stories see: www.once-online.com

DANIELLE MCLAUGHLIN's stories have appeared in *The Stinging Fly*, *Long Story Short*, the *Irish Times*, *The Burning Bush 2*, *Inktears*, *Southword*, *Boyne Berries*, *Crannóg*, *Hollybough*, in various anthologies, and on radio. She won the Writing Spirit Award for Fiction 2010, the From the Well Short Story Competition 2012, the William Trevor/ Elizabeth Bowen International Short Story Competition 2012, the Willesden Herald Short Story Competition 2012–2013 and the Merriman Short Story Competition in memory of Maeve Binchy.

PAUL MCMAHON, from Belfast, Ireland, holds an MA in Writing, with first class honours, from NUIG, Ireland. His poetry has been widely published in journals such as *The Threepenny Review* and *Southword*. He won first prize in The Ballymaloe International Poetry Prize (2012), The Nottingham Poetry Open Competition (2012), The Westport Arts Festival Poetry Competition (2012) and in The Golden Pen Poetry Prize (2011). He received a literature bursary award from the Arts Council of Ireland in 2013.

C. S. MEE is from Birkenhead and currently lives in Switzerland. She recently completed an MA in Creative Writing with Lancaster University. Her fiction has appeared in *Prole* and *Wasafiri*. Her story 'The Walk' won the *Wasafiri* New Writing Prize 2012 and 'Fugit Amor' was placed third in the Neil Gunn Writing Competition 2013. She is working on a novel.

JAY MERILL is the winner of the Salt Short Story Prize with her story 'As Birds Fly'. Her two recent short story collections *God of the Pigeons* and *Astral Bodies* (both Salt), were nominated for the Frank O'Connor Award and Edge Hill Prize. She is writing a novel assisted by an award from Arts Council England and is Writer in Residence at Women in Publishing.

ALBAN MILES grew up in London and worked first in book publishing; after a year living and working in Hong Kong, he returned as a teacher. He has always written, but only recently managed to finish anything. He lives in London.

MATTHEW MORGAN was born in Bristol in 1985. He has a degree in Sociology and an MA in Creative Writing. He's currently writing his first novel. He also volunteers as an arts worker at Art and Power and he's the editor of the online literary magazine *Éclat Fiction*.

PEARSE MURRAY has had several poems and short stories published in a variety of on-line, print journals and anthologies. He was one of the award winners in The Lonely Voice series sponsored by the Irish Writers

Centre. He is a native of Dublin and lives in upstate New York.

REBECCA PERRY is a graduate of Manchester's Centre for New Writing and currently lives in London. Her poetry has appeared most recently in *Poetry London*, *The Rialto* and *Best British Poetry 2013*. Her pamphlet, *little armoured*, published by Seren in 2012, won the Poetry Wales Purple Moose Prize and was a Poetry Book Society Choice.

JONATHAN PINNOCK has had over a hundred stories and poems published in places both illustrious and downright insalubrious. He has also won a few prizes and has had work broadcast on the BBC. His debut novel *Mrs Darcy versus the Aliens* was published by Proxima Books in September 2011, and his Scott Prize-winning debut collection of short stories, *Dot Dash*, was published by Salt in November 2012. He blogs at www.jonathanpinnock.com and he tweets as @jonpinnock.

DAN POWELL is a full-time father and part-time teacher. His short fiction has featured in *Carve*, *Paraxis* and *The Best British Short Stories 2012*. He recently won a Carve Esoteric Award and was shortlisted for the 2013 Scott Prize. His debut collection of short fiction will be published by Salt in 2014 and he is currently working on a novel. He procrastinates at danpowellfiction.com

ALLIE ROGERS was born in Brighton in 1970 where she lives and works as a librarian. Allie writes all types of fiction. She was shortlisted for the Fish Flash Fiction Prize in 2012 and has had stories published in *The Yellow Room* magazine.

CHERISE SAYWELL grew up in Australia and has lived in the UK for fifteen years. She is the author of two novels, *Twitcher* and *Desert Fish*. She won the V.S. Pritchett Memorial Prize in 2003 and was a runner-up in the Asham Award in 2009. She lives in Edinburgh with her partner and their two children.

AIDAN SEMMENS is a freelance journalist and blogger, who may occasionally be encountered in the sports pages of *The Independent*. He is the author of two poetry collections, *A Stone Dog* (Shearsman 2011), and *The Book of Isaac* (Parlor Press 2013), which was shortlisted by Salt for the Crashaw Prize. He is also the editor of an anthology of Suffolk poetry, *By The North Sea* (Shearsman 2013), and of *Molly Bloom*, an online magazine of innovative poetry (www.mollybloom.org.uk).

JOSE VARGHESE works as an Assistant Professor of English. He is the chief editor of *Lakeview International Journal of Literature and Arts*. His poems and stories have already appeared in reputed journals/anthologies. New works this year will be in *Unthology* and the Red Squirrel Anthology *10RED*. He is invited for the 13th International Conference on the Short Story in English in Vienna. He is the author of *Silver-Painted Gandhi And Other Poems* and his forthcoming book is *Silent Woman and Other Stories*.

JUDI WALSH was born in Hertford and grew up in Norfolk. After studying in Birmingham, she returned to Norwich where she lives with her family. *Victor* is her first print publication.

ADAM WILSHAW was a senior reporter on the *Western Morning News* and *North Devon Journal*. He quit journalism in 2011 and moved with his wife and two very young children to Alcaniz, a small town in the wild and beautiful Spanish province of Teruel, where he taught English and wrote a surreal literary novel inspired by the economic crisis. In 2012 he moved to Figueres to teach English and finish his second novel. *Flowers, Whisky* is his first published fiction.

NICHOLAS YH WONG is a Malaysian poet based in Chicago, Illinois. He is a recipient of two Academy of American Poets Awards and the Arthur E. Ford Poetry Prize, and his poems have appeared in *The Rialto, Columbia Review, Southeast Asian Review of English* and other journals. He is a PhD student in Comparative Literature at the University of Chicago and a poetry staff at Chicago Review.

JANWOOLF.COM is an activist/writer/producer. Her collection of stories *Fugues on a Funny Bone* (Muswell-Press) and her play *Porn Crackers* (based on her past as teacher and film censor) emerged during her Harold Pinter writers' residency at the Hackney Empire, 2010. Her recent play *You Don't Know What You Don't Know* (Royal Court 2013) was part of TEN for Stop the War. She is active in the Writers Guild of Great Britain and runs *Off the Shelf* at Black's club, Soho.

JANE YEH's first collection of poems, *Marabou* (2005), was shortlisted for the Whitbread, Forward, and Aldeburgh poetry prizes. Her latest collection, *The Ninjas*, was published by Carcanet in 2012. She teaches creative writing at Kingston University London, and on Arvon's residential courses.

Also by Salt

LIMERICK CITY LIBRARY

Phone: 407510
Website:
www.limerickcity.ie/library
Email: citylib@limerickcity.ie

The Gran
Michael St
Limerick.

**This book is issued subject to the Rules of the Library.
The Book mu be returned not later then the last dat
stamped below.**